Damien Wilkins is one of New Zealand's leading writers. He is the author of short stories, poetry and seven novels, including the New Zealand Book Award-winning *The Miserables* and *The Fainter*, which was shortlisted for both the Montana New Zealand Book Awards and the Commonwealth Writers Prize. He lives in Wellington, where he is the Director of the International Institute of Modern Letters at Victoria University.

D0063153

ALSO BY DAMIEN WILKINS

The Veteran Perils (short stories)

The Miserables

The Idles (poems)

Little Masters

Nineteen Widows Under Ash

When Famous People Come to Town (essay)

Chemistry

Great Sporting Moments (as editor)

The Fainter

For Everyone Concerned (short stories)

Somebody Loves Us All

MAX GATE

AARDVARK
BUREAU

Praise for *Chemistry*

'A terrifically good book, so cleverly constructed and managed. It's a work of real tenderness…powerful and convincing.'
Jim Crace

'Wilkins is brilliant at character…the writing is full of verve. Wilkins has an eye for telling detail, a great ear for dialogue and a dark sense of humour. It is easy to understand the acclaim he has already won in his native New Zealand.'
Guardian

Praise for *Little Masters*

'*Little Masters* is an engrossing, fiercely readable book. It deals with classic themes of parents and children, love and exile, and the sadness of separation and dislocation. Damien Wilkins writes brilliantly about streetwise, smart children and adults searching for love and stability far away from home.'
Colm Tóibín

Praise for *The Miserables*

'Wilkins has constructed a powerful portrait of family life… He handles the temporal shifts of the narrative with delicacy, precision, remarkable grace and apparent lack of effort…the prose is controlled, elegant, almost deadpan…A moving and subtle piece of work.'
Times Literary Supplement

MAX GATE

DAMIEN WILKINS

A NOVEL

Aardvark Bureau
London

An Aardvark Bureau Book
An imprint of Gallic Books

First published by Victoria University Press, New Zealand, 2013
Copyright © Damien Wilkins, 2013

Damien Wilkins has asserted his moral right to be identified as the
author of the work.

First published in Great Britain in 2016 by
Aardvark Bureau, 59 Ebury Street,
London, SW1W 0NZ

A CIP record for this book is available from the British Library
ISBN 978-1-910709-13-9

Typeset in Garamond Pro by Aardvark Bureau
Printed in the UK by CPI (CR0 4YY)
2 4 6 8 10 9 7 5 3 1

for Bill Manhire

'Small boys write to him from New Zealand
and have to be answered.'

from Virginia Woolf's diaries

PART ONE

When you wake in a warm bed in winter besieged all around by cold, for an instant you believe you have it in your power to stay right where you are for as long as you want.

Downstairs, the dog barks. He'll be at the master's door, puzzled and afraid, and looking forward to biting the postman.

But of course you don't have that power. Someone wants you, or your life does.

The dog's misery was all of ours. Hear him howl!

Some mornings I think Wessex will burrow through the carpet and right under the door. He's already made a terrible mess of the wood, pawing and leaning his teeth into it.

I try to block everything out, get another few minutes, but at Max Gate sleeping is its own insulation and fools you into believing the bed is a haven. The blankets are not that good after all. Nothing in the house is. The attic rooms which cook in summer, now collect the chill air through gaps in the roof no one is interested in fixing since it's only us two girls who climb the stairs each day, on our way to heaven of course…And Alice through the wall is banging about. 'Hey yup,' she calls.

'Hey yup,' I call out.

'Thac bleeding dog.'

'Thiccy, thaccy, thic! You need to go down and turn on the radio for him.'

They didn't even bother to hook a wire up here but

downstairs the dog has his own radio and a chair for listening in. For an hour or so, he's calm under the music and voices. The electricity, source of great suspicion for Mr Hardy, ends below us. Beside my bed are little mounds of candle-wax which some nights I chip at in the dark with my fingernail.

Remember the time we built a roaring fire downstairs to welcome Mrs Florence back one night she'd been without him to London. We found him on hands and knees with a pair of tongs removing individual coals from the grate as a saving.

I swing my feet from the bed. There's so much cold the floor feels damp. At the window, I can just see over the tops of the trees dotted with snow. In another year, it won't be possible. Not that we're likely to have another year. This height, I always tell Alice, is our one reward. Denied even to Mrs Florence, who must wade about below us, shadowed and shaded. Last month I asked her was there anything else I could bring her.

An axe, she said.

An axe, Alice and I say to each other after a bad day, an axe! Bring me an axe, would you.

Through the thin wall, Alice Riglar farts good morning: her usual sharp balloonish sound, pinched and complaining. She is from Rimpton Mill, apparently near Yeovil—I'll take her word for it—across the border in Somerset, where her father is a baker. She's a yeasty girl, apple-cheeked, fond of Dorset knobs, the dry biscuit we claim as our contribution to the culinary arts, and she often angles for the ride into town to get Mr Hardy's order—though it's more properly, in the all-rolled-up-into-one manner of Max Gate where

Cook says everyone does everything though Cook herself does only what's strictly required and sometimes squeezes out of that too, the parlour-maid's circuit. In exchange with Alice, who's a between-maid, I'll do the mail by bicycle to South Street, giving me a chance to look in on my mother for a few minutes.

I take a breath and splash the nightstand water on my face. I must have cried out too because Alice is at the door.

'Jesus, Nellie Titterington,' she says, 'ye yell out, I thought you was entertaining.'

'I'm very entertaining.'

'It's what I heard.'

'I'm famous, am I?'

Is it mention of famous that makes us stop?

'Anyone come to the house in the night?' I say.

'I weren't called,' she says.

'Nor me.'

'Business as usual then. Mr Cockerell here this morning and the Barrie maybe in the evening.'

'Right,' I tell her, 'then shake a leg.'

She hitches her nightdress and kicks me on the shin.

Some nights recently Alice has been overtaken by weeping and I go in. What are you crying about? Not him below us, I hope? No, she cries. Good, I say. Anyway, I know your problem. What is it? Not enough Dorset knobs. It's an old joke between us. Alice's chap has been away since before Christmas, visiting family somewhere in the North. Can one lose one's taste for it? she says. Never heard of it before. Changing the supplier is usually the remedy. She laughs but is immediately unhappy again and grasps my hand. Promise you won't go, Nellie. When the master

15

dies, promise me you won't go. But Alice knows as well as me, it won't be in our choosing. Once he's gone, I tell her again, it'll be every man, woman, cat, dog and hedgehog for himself. Alice buries her head and speaks into the pillow. And if she chooses you to go with her, which she will, she says, I know you'll take the offer and why wouldn't you since it'll mean London. I'd take it myself in a flash. And it'll be farewell Alice, nice knowing you, I know it will. Sweet, I say, nothing's decided and nothing's for sure. For one, the master might sit up today and say, what are you all mooching around for, bring me my slippers! She looks up. Really? I don't know, I say. No one does, and that's the beauty of the thing. Oh, Nell, there's nothing beautiful and if you think so, you're stupider than me, which can't be true, so you're a liar and I'm doomed. Comb my hair, will ye?

She has lovely hair, thick and almost golden, and a pain to comb. Sit up then, I tell her.

Alice and I like each other enough to confide, though she's wary of me finally and I understand this. She's twenty and on the make. I'm the older one but not so much older I don't get mistaken for her age and in a toss-up between us, my talents at this stage are greater. I can write and read to a good standard, and I can speak acceptably. In addition I'm Mrs Florence's own—she treats me sometimes as a friend, though not of course like a real friend. Alice is astonishing with her hands. Sewed her many sisters' clothes since she was nine years old. In the future, if not right now, we are competitors. She envies me my mind while not especially seeing its value, and this can make her sullen and less articulate with her employers than she could be and less appealing than her basically sunny nature equips her to be.

With confidence she'll grow, but we both sense this won't happen until we're apart. Somehow I'm standing in her light. Meanwhile we have great fun and are regularly saved by each other's company.

On clear nights we struggle through the attic window and perch, smoking, like convicts on the roof of a prison taking a break from the riot below.

The morning dark is beginning to lift and from the window I see Bert Stephens, the only one of us not sleeping here, enter the garden by the rear gate, keys in hand. For that moment he looks like our jailer, checking our number, making sure no one's escaped in the night.

Better that we had.

Alice is at my side, peering out too. The snow is light on the lawn. She smells nice somehow. Of—butter? 'What's ugly and has the head of a mushroom?' she says.

'Shush,' I say, 'Bert's all right.'

'Who said that's the correct answer. Wasn't talking about Bert at all, was I.' And she pokes me in the ribs so I double over. 'Christ ye need to wash your neck.' She's sweeping my hair off and touching the patch.

'Reach it for me,' I say, giving her the wet cloth, and she does.

'What will happen with you and Alex?' she says.

I speak from under my hair. 'It's over.'

'A man makes one mistake and it's over?'

'And then a woman makes a mistake back at him.'

'"The Fellow I Met in Town",' says Alice.

'Him.'

'Then you're even, not over.' She drops the cloth beside me. 'And you're clean, or as near as you'll get at Max Gate.'

We didn't know this yet but he was biking towards us at that moment, through the mushy wooded sections along the road from town. Mr Alexander Peters, who was killed in the War eleven years later. I suppose you could say we were expecting something and he was to bring it to us that day, as any postman would a package, though he didn't have a firm idea of what and nor did anyone. He wears his trousers clipped, and his cheeks are numb in the wind. On the straight he lets go of the handlebars and tucks his hands under his armpits, riding free, casting a clean and fizzing line behind him in the shallow snow. Oh Alex. He wrote for the paper and was hoping for a scoop or to be involved somehow. When Old Tom dies, he told me, I'm first there. Will you help me? Will you help me, my darling Nell? And I said I would, I would. But now—. His bike disappears from view, his red panniers. A few seconds after, a squirrel runs across the road, stopping in the middle, listening to the wheels on the road, trying to know what manner of animal was coming.

Above Alex, at St. Michael's, a couple of heavy old sheep wandering among the little falling-down railings, eating the grass where it poked through in frosty blades, nibbling the graves. The bicycle passed them without notice. A time later, the sounds of a car engine make the sheep look up. Then a V in the air, and sensing it, little fellows further in duck away, enter their holes.

It was the taxi from the station, bringing Mr Cockerell to us again. He too coming fatefully, like a messenger. He was sitting in the back, reading the paper.

Think we'll see the sun today?

No, sir.

Mr Cockerell wouldn't know this but there was a saucer by the door of the same church. Reverend Cowley bends down and then stands up again, with a jug. He's seen the bicycle and the car. It's the place where all the Hardys are buried: father and mother, his beloved sister, and Emma, his first wife. For seven hundred years people have been coming along the lanes to pray. Some of the original parishioners are still in attendance, Alice reckons. Reverend Cowley makes a kissing sound with his lips, and dead-still waits, peering across the whitened grass. Puss, puss, puss, he kisses. Nothing happens and then after the door is shut, it appears. Feline revenants passing over the heath, by the river, under the bridges, as cautious and quick as spiders. This cat lives with others in the wild. They are the sort who visit us also, crying under the windows, expecting to be thrown scraps, descendants no doubt of the animals fed by the original Mrs Hardy, who was a crazy cat woman. A photo I found in a drawer—and not one put out ever— shows her, cat on either side, hair wild as if she's been rolling with them some place. And on her face, a hostile look, like that of a child interrupted in a game.

An axe, say the freezing maids, and maybe a pair of revolvers, if you don't mind.

Actually, Mrs Florence has a revolver in the drawer of her bedroom dresser. She had it for the nights of her first years of marriage when she was often left alone and feared intruders, folk coming through the trees, soundlessly through the swaying branches on a windy night—I tell Alice stories on the roof too. Look in the trees! Where? Don't you see it?

Meanwhile at Max Gate, we are waiting, trying to live the normal day. But if everyone in a house gets up and yet there's still one who can't, then it's impossible.

I've cleared the ashes.

Chamber pots.

New coal in.

Curtains.

Guest bedrooms.

Oil lamps. Oil lamps!

I've filled the jugs.

Passed Cook staring grumpily into the fire in the kitchen. Where's the heat in this thing? You could put your hand in there and not be scalded. Go on then, I said.

Upstairs again. Knock, knock. But Mrs Florence was ahead of me. I knew where she was.

She was in his study, opening the curtains, a job she's always taken for herself. Good, I don't need another.

She'd open them and leave quickly. But this time she pauses and looks across at his writing desk, where he's worked all these years. There are neat piles of paper on the desk. He is neat and demands it of us, often without care of tone would be the polite way of saying that. She finds herself tidying the perfect piles. Pointless! She is prone to that word herself. Things are, we are, she is, life is—. The first we knew her, she was not where she is today. The fact won't let her settle into giving orders with any naturalness. She is not natural. Which creates this strange connection we have—what am I to her exactly? She can't decide if I'm 'Nellie' or Nellie. She relies on me but also pays me— the paying spoils the reliance, each tenderness seemingly purchased. Yet I'm not compelled to be interested in her.

I just am. She touches the back of his chair and hesitates. She pulls the chair out as if to, hesitates once more. She presses her fingers against her temples as if something in there wants out. But she won't let it. She won't let it.

In the hall she's met her younger sister Eva who came last week and will stay now until—until she isn't needed. Eva has told her the night was very comfortable for Tom. She sleeps in the small room next to his and gets up every hour or so to check on him. Six months ago Eva had come to nurse him through a threatening flu. Her presence at Max Gate therefore isn't final in any way. She's been with worse patients, she tells Florence, who've pulled through. It doesn't sound false in Eva's flat delivery. She's incapable of cheeriness to an almost comical degree. Yet her steady uninflected voice gives an even beat to a rhythm that seems mostly out-of-step. Funny that when they were girls this voice so riled Florence, who considered it an affectation. But Eva turned out exactly as she promised and Florence finds these brief reports strangely helpful even at the moment she's inwardly rejecting them, just as she's discovered to her amazement that the mere sound of her sister's tread on the carpet is consoling and not, as she feared, infuriating. She watches herself listening to her sister, waiting to explode, feeling the sparkle of a lit fuse run along the insides of her arms, and somehow the fuse ends in her shoulders, which slump in a sort of self-comfort.

Below the window, on Mr Hardy's age-old orders, his warm command, the hare feeds freely in the remarkably resilient vegetable patch, watching Cook pull carrots from the hard ground.

Bert Stephens is forbidden to shoot the hare.

Cook pretends sometimes to forget and calls her Miss Dugdale, just at the edge of hearing. What was that they said? Florence will turn slightly but she won't ask us— to ask would be to invite the old undermining thoughts. How they hate me, she must think, no matter what I do for them or how I behave. And what for? For improving my position. Cook recites the history for anyone new. This Florence was not much more than a girl when she first came to Max Gate to be his secretary, young enough to be his granddaughter, and here she is, having written her way into the story line by line, just as the borer beetle eats through the floor.

Occasionally I've made reassuring noises which Mrs Florence ignores. She knows by asking me to tell her what is said about her, she's asking me to lie and at once this irritates her.

Do they fuck? Alice always puts into words what everyone's thinking so everyone can deny they ever had it in mind. Can't imagine it, she says.

Imagine away, I've said to her. Opinion was the master took more on the deal than Mrs Florence did. Though one Christmas she went around us all and made up our bonuses to ten shillings from his measly outlay and told us not to tell. I think that was a happy Christmas for her, the year before you came, Alice. Just my luck, she says. But, Nell, next time you're dusting and she's bent over, dust in there for us and we'll all thank you for it.

Alice jokes but seethes too—how else to battle the unfairness of a world in which she—an attractive, open, available person—has somehow been locked up in a uniform and a house which belongs to an earlier era of ugliness and secrets. The days of Service are coming to an end—we know it—but we must all pretend this is not the case, just as we must pretend there's a chance Thomas Hardy will, any day now, sit up in his bed and feel better.

Yet he is not Old Tom now. Thomas *Hardly* is what Alex calls him. Will you help me, my love? Will ye? Alex was ruthless too, I must remember. Or if that feels too harsh and I think it does, he was avaricious. He had an appetite—for food, for experiences—and I've always liked such people and suspected people who are moderate, though I am moderate. I've never liked people who eat slowly, though how often did I hear myself telling Jenny to slow down. Really I enjoyed her need. Obviously it meant I was connected to her since it was food I'd prepared that she shovelled down.

Had Florence Hardy wanted children at one point? Cook says yes, but he didn't want them, was too old, and probably it was for the best, Cook thinks. She's in receipt of a story about an alkaline douche but neither Alice nor I wish to know more. It's generally good to thwart Cook.

Mrs Florence is at the bottom desk drawer and slowly opens it, taking out a battered cardboard shoebox. Unsure what to do next. Then she hears the dog barking. This brings her around. She returns the box to the drawer, pushes the chair in again and leaves, stumbling once as she goes and looking back at the carpet, as if some object has surprised her. What sort of thing? She has the temperament that sees malevolence everywhere. It's an ageing outlook. She appears much older than fifty. When I comb her hair I think of my mother, who is sixty-five and who regards herself in the mirror with sternness and disapproval, swiftly. Mrs Florence, too, will look away and only flick her eyes in the direction of her image, a quick check. Presentable.

Wessex was at the front gate again, a very excitable animal. Warning someone off, jumping at something. Cook says the dog was one of two items Mrs Florence introduced into the house—the other was her pianola, which he has forbidden her to play on account of the noise. The noise of Wessex he is used to, has given in to, requires now. He loves Wessex as she does, maybe more. It is the single wildness he allows. The dog, I think, is where they have stored whatever first attracted them to each other, what heat they generated he carries in his biting mouth and when he leaps, they think, oh *that*.

I'd stepped out to beat the rug. A plume of dust rises, and there's misty rain above the sprinkled trees.

You ran under the trees and it poured on you, right down your neck. Once I stood under there with him and a wet leaf fell on his head. What do we know of these? he asked me, holding it out. A leaf veined as a hand. The veins of his smallish hands. Then he told me the order in which leaves fall is usually this, though not every November: Chestnuts, Sycamores, Limes, Hornbeams, Elm, Birch, Beech. Get wet or get a lecture—our choices! I looked at his hands, no more than a boy's size. In other houses you knew you were in for a groping but to him it was as if we weren't quite real. He looked, sometimes gazed and gazed, but didn't touch. He could come alive with young women. His eyes electric and searching, yet just as quickly dulled again, as if he'd decided that what he thought and hoped was present, wasn't. Here was Florence Hardy's pain—at one time she'd been the cause of the electric current. Perhaps it had lasted a little longer than with others. But now she was—like us. Women weren't really there. Or we existed as a single entity. Did he know just a single female—his mother or sisters, or some little girl from his childhood? Many men are like this after all. We are just shapes to fill in a jigsaw and if we don't fit—.

'Quiet!' I said. 'Wessex, quiet now. No one's there, you silly dog. Quiet.'

I look up at the window of Mr Hardy's bedroom, where the curtains are shut, then notice Mrs Florence at the window of the study, looking down at me.

Wessex, of course, was their child.

Poor creatures. Dogs can sense these things, can't they, the sadness, the anxiety and fear and the event happening. Whatever one hoped, it was coming. Alex on his bike. Mr Cockerell in his car. Mrs Florence with her shoebox. The Barrie later. Even Alice with her tears. And me?

Death is dreadful, full of dread. I dread it. I cannot imagine the thing which is so plainly happening in front of our eyes. An old man loving, craving someone nearly forty years his junior—that's easy to imagine anywhere, any time. But not this. Away from Alice, I was terrified, squeamish, and my hands trembled as I wound the big clock in the hall. In winding it, I was, for a moment, stopping the mechanism. The clicking of seconds was paused. In this pause I imagined him dying. For the past three days now, when I wind, I wait longer and longer beside the silenced thing, listening to the house, creating the gap for the worst to occur, delaying the return of time. For I believe one dies in a special space, uncertain, immeasurable, beyond time. There is no 'time of death'. So I wait, holding the advance of the next ordinary moment. But of course on closing the glass door, the clock starts again. It breathes out.

Oh why did I care for him? In no way is he a father or even friendly much. I'm invisible, or visible only as image of some ghost-girl, a piece of his past he looks for everywhere and can't recover. Yet over these four years I've somehow become part of it all, another stone in the path, in the damp wall.

I patted the stone dog as I went up the steps. This was the statue by the front door, paws in the air. And whenever Mr Hardy entered Max Gate, he'd touch the head. Good boy. Give him a rub, he'd say to whomever was the following person, the Prime Minister, the Prince of Wales, a wife, a great poet, it didn't matter. And you always found yourself obeying, no matter who you were. You rubbed that head.

What do you call him? some would ask Mr Hardy.

Eh?

What's his name, Tom?

Name? he'd reply. Those quizzical bright eyes, the long head he rested unexpectedly having said something, putting it down shyly like some old pointer pigeon. The trotting walk. But it's a statue, what would be the purpose? He'd never come if I called.

It was cold even in summertime, the pocked head, the ears speckled in lichen. I brush a blob of snow off.

Look up on the doorstep before going in and what do we see? Red bricks, bushy creepers, tangled ivy. Windows chopped into small panes. It's a fine house, respectable, hard to clean, cold, damp, cold. Mr Hardy doesn't believe in conveniences. He's old-fashioned. Or just old—yet he was always this way. His father and brother made the house; he liked to say this often, touching the brick. Proud. But Mrs Florence told me they argued so much that the father and brother vowed never to work for Tom again and never did. They argued over materials. Over money. They argued over the meanness and impracticality of the design (Tom's own).

Do you know how much water weighs when collected for his hip bath? And we must lug it up the narrow stairs. Already I'm too broad in the shoulders, too full in the calves. Like some upright pony or donkey. My wrists are granite! Jesus, I can scare a man with just my walk. The Fellow I Met in Town I could have carried over my shoulder but I was careful to pretend he was overpowering. That I was under his spell. Is it what she must pretend too?

And then with the Fellow, I couldn't stop myself. I brought my thighs together on his pale thin flanks and pressed. He squealed. Why had I done it? Shortly he was gathering up his clothes, inventing the urgency of a young wife due back, when his two rooms showed nothing of her touch. I almost laughed in his face. We were both drunk. The walls seemed to echo his squeal. You're dry, he said, whining. You're too small, I told him. He murmured that he'd had no previous complaints. I'd like to know the survey numbers, I said. On second thought, I said, I've never met a man who didn't prefer a larger number to the actual one. You seem to have known plenty yourself, he said. He was in his trousers now, which gave him a body by hiding his. Don't worry, I told him, I won't be counting you. Then I walked three miles home in the dark, kicking at the grass to warn things off and because it felt better than not doing it.

I hate the house. Bring me an axe! Where is my revolver?

One day I came across Mr Hardy standing at the doorway, looking into the room which was shown to visitors. As if he were a visitor, marvelling at the man he was about to meet, which would have been himself, logically. The room contains only books written by him, and only pictures on the wall drawn by him or by others from those books, and other artifacts connected with him. Copies of the Roman stuff they found digging the foundations. The Hardy Museum we called it. Gloomy and correct and inspected for the smallest mote, the tiniest streak. I said, excuse me, sir. He did not move but spoke, not quite to me, 'The worst of taking a furnished house is that the articles in the rooms are saturated with the thoughts and glances of others.'

I said, 'I like others myself.' And he looked at me very fiercely with his moustache and walked off. At that moment: wrong sort of ghost-girl completely.

The torn-looking trees, the hare eating the glassy crisp lettuce where it stands.

Years after I left, it was still happening, dreams of Max Gate, dreams of the trees, our little rooms above it all. What falls first—Beech or Birch? And is he still leaping, that nameless stone dog? Or is he eaten half away?

*

Then came a crash. That noise was Alex, organising his bicycle.

He used to bring us things he'd shot, leaving them on the back step. It was how we first met. I thought he was the butcher's boy, seeing him disappearing and I called to him. 'You!' I called. 'Boy!' It was what I called him later too. Boy! Even though he was older than me. And sometimes he called me ma'am and tickled me under the ribs—men who tickle. It's as if we are their chums. I saw it just the other day, a boy and girl on the street; he tickling and she shrieking. It must be an eternal pattern.

Cook had been a friend of Alex's mother.

And next the sound of the taxi. Mr Cockerell getting out, carrying an umbrella and his small overnight bag. He had other things already in the room upstairs. Shirts, shoes. Alice has ironed them, polished. Must have the Cock looking good.

Bert Stephens sticks his head out from the garden shed. 'The hordes are descending.'

'Looks like it,' I say.

'Anyone come last night?'

'No,' I say.

'The doctor?'

'Usual visit later, I suppose, Bert.'

'Humpf,' he says. His father and Mr Hardy were boys together. The latter's longevity seems to count against him with Bert. He also enjoys telling the story of his father and his schoolboy pals eating their sandwiches under a railway arch, then one of them throwing young Tom's cap into the doorway of a shop. When Tom went to retrieve it, an old woman called Sally Warren came at him with a broom.

29

'Sally Warren was a great ballywrag and didn't miss with her spanking!' Sometimes, after Mr Hardy instructs Bert in a matter and walks off a safe distance, Bert raises his arms as if to swing an imaginary broom at him. He also likes to drop the word 'spanking' into conversation with the master: 'Yes, sir, I'll give those leaves a good spanking and no mistake!' Connected with this half-buried rivalry and hatched with Mrs Florence, there's a conspiracy going back years to prune as many branches as possible without the master realising. Bert remembers when the house was built on a rise bare as a baby's head. I've seen the photograph. Now Mr Hardy can't get up to see what's going on, and is past taking an interest, the secret pruning has stopped. Why play a game when the opposition has gone home? Why throw a cap if the boy won't retrieve it?

Bert retreats inside again.

I fold the rug over my muscled forearm. I could take Alex in an arm-wrestle. Not that I'll give him the chance, nor he me. The thought makes my pelvis clench. I do love his body and mine.

So the day begins when we try to hear it all and try not to listen, pulled and pushed. It is January 10th, 1928 on the calendar that Cook looks at for dates of dinners, visitors. Whatever is learned, we share. The falling apart pieced together. The animals in their movements, the voices, the birds in their feeder, tiny dents in the wood from their beaks.

He named Max Gate after an ancient tollgate at the Fordington end of Dorchester. Even though the house was new, he wanted it old immediately. If he could have built a ruin, he would have done it and set us all up in it, as working models of servants from forgotten ages, bringing him his meals, winding his clocks, wind-ups ourselves, reminding him of some other figures moving through immemorial, crumbling landscapes.

At one time, in the second year of my service I believe, five owls were roosting in the trees and it was one of our duties to fetch Mr Hardy should we spy them. In his winter coat and little black felt hat and red scarf, he would stand beneath the branches as owlish as them, as unmoving and as moved. Until it came to the attention of Mrs Florence who ordered us never to fetch the master unless we wanted to see an old man carried off not by owls but by pneumonia. He is prone to colds.

Yet she used to watch him too, the first times. I saw her do it. At the window she was, and looking out at him looking at the owls looking at him or perhaps the owls were looking at nothing but shapes, the shape of an old man in a hat in front of the shape of a house, as if they were collecting pieces themselves from pasts we can't know about—likely, isn't it, that others had done the same as this old man: tried to see into their owl natures. But their natures, like ours, are folded up inside, like wings, and live in the thickest branches, dressed in leaves.

The hare sees the two men and takes a different path, hopping behind a tree. I imagine it carries a recording device attached to one ear, which I placed there so that my account could be as full as possible.

Why am I hearing gunfire?

'There's urgency then, Mr Cockerell? With Mr Hardy.' The reporter is finding his pen and notebook from his coat pocket.

'Naturally, Peters. Mr Hardy is a writer. Everything presses on that specimen.' Mr Cockerell reaches for the gate handle.

'Only my sources suggest a seriousness beyond the usual pressures of such a trying occupation.'

Mr Cockerell turns and looks at Alex. 'Who are you with again?'

'*Dorset County Chronicle*, sir.'

'Have the nationals been about at all?'

'I like to have the jump, sir.'

'Do you indeed?'

I want somehow to say—to whom? to myself?— that this remembering, this story, is not mine exactly but belongs to everyone who was involved with the house. I want sometimes to say 'we' but that's presumptuous since no one else is agreeing with the way I remember and see things. (Besides, old person, you are asleep.) Anyway. Everyone liked Alex, some more than others. He knows the woodlands and heath as well as anybody. Good with a pen usually discounts practical skill, yet Alex could catch a fish and set a trap. Cook said he had a kind face and that he got it from his dear mother, yet it's the face I can't quite picture now, which is strange given that I held it in my hands often and brought it close to mine—probably though that's not a position from which we can accurately reconstruct features. The beloved looms and we push ourselves into it to smother its power or to share its power or to match our power against it. His nose was running from the bike ride and he wiped it with his sleeve. How wrong that he was killed. I don't say it selfishly, that I was robbed, that I was the only sufferer but I am one of them. I am in that line.

A note flares up: Robert's face. (Certainly you are asleep.)

Alex continues: 'In a way he belongs to us is my feeling, which is only to say I stand in for the loyalty of the district. This is Hardy country, after all. He's named us, Mr Cockerell, as any guidebook will tell it.'

'Hardy country, it's true,' says Mr Cockerell. 'But let's not be too quick at ownership. He belongs to everyone, I'd say. And I'd hope, Peters, what you write might include some appropriate phrasing…let's see…"Adored by the nation, Thomas Hardy, the esteemed and beloved author of many novels, including imperishably *Tess of the—*"'

'We have an obit filed, sir. It was more the time and circumstances and witnesses, if any. The human side. The nation, as much as folk about, will want to be satisfied on the scale of some details, no matter how maudlin, Mr Cockerell. I don't want to think it, let alone say it but is Mr Hardy gone, sir?'

'Not yet, Peters. Not yet.'

'Ah, I'm happy to hear it. I had a terrible feeling biking here but it was probably just the cold. And the fact my chain needs oiling.'

'Well I warn you that there's a small dog about too. Bites everyone except his master and mistress, and once ate the meat off Lady Fitzgerald's fork—with impunity. I saw it myself, the dog walked the length of the table to get it.'

'That would be Wessex, sir.'

Mr Cockerell has the gate open. The reporter peers inside. The breathing of both men comes in brief clouds through the thick cold. Bottle it now!

'Yet my sources suggest the great author is—'

'I tell you Tom lives still, Mr Peters, no matter your sources. He survives amidst the placidities of his beautiful Dorset home where for many years he has brought the world to his feet. And short of asking you to accompany me into his bedroom to poke him with your pen, I fear there's probably no chance of other persuasion. Good day, sir. And when the sad and mighty event transpires, God forbid, make sure your obit is corrected mercilessly, especially in the matter of titles, book titles. Tom loathed proofing errors. We are talking about a custodian of the language. It is not "*June* the Obscure", as I have seen it before, and it is not "The Return *Home* of the Native". Have you read any of the above works?'

'Me? I'm a regular bookworm, sir. Why they sent me down here. Is the lady of the house available for comment, given your hurry?'

Mr Cockerell shuts the gate behind him. He turns back immediately and speaks through the railings. 'The lady is not to be approached. You must understand that, Peters. Her husband lies gravely ill. What "comment" could there usefully be from such a source? Please come through me for your information. Does the *Dorset Messenger* carry a good photo of Mr Hardy?'

'*Chronicle*, sir.' Alex is writing in his notebook. 'I shall check, sir. "Gravely", I have it. You're an intimate and I prize that view you offer. She's distressed?'

'Who? Florence?'

'"Bearing up" perhaps. What would you write?'

'Oh, let's see. "Stoic".'

Alex speaks as he writes. '"The stoic Mrs Hardy sits by the great man's bedside."'

Mr Cockerell opens the gate, takes a few steps towards Alex so he is at his elbow, looking at what he writes.

'Reading to him?' says Alex. He knows this already of course since I've told him. For years now, Mrs Florence has read to Mr Hardy at night. The bookmark is not to be dislodged. Alex knew a lot before I came on the scene, but I added things.

'Taking comfort in the classics, is better still,' says Mr Cockerell, indicating with his gloved finger on the reporter's notebook.

'"Comfort in the classics. The vigil is unbroken."'

'I'm encouraging her to have breaks.'

'"Unmindful of her own needs."'

'She fusses somewhat, always has. Her nature is that kind of devotion. A worrier. Don't...write that. She is many years his junior and behaves in certain ways as a daughter to him, in the style of reprimands and so forth. Plus she has herself not been very well.'

Mr Cockerell looks up at us in the house, then back again. How many faces has he seen? The house with eyes. The hare is still.

'That your bicycle, Peters? Only it might be best if it were not parked quite there.'

'I'll be gone presently, sir.'

35

'We are unfortunately gathering ourselves for an invasion of the press.'

'With me having the jump, sir.'

'You're keen, Peters, I'll give you that.'

The reporter puts away his notebook and stamps his feet to get the feeling going.

'Tom, as well as being a dog-lover, was, is a great cyclist of course,' says Mr Cockerell.

'I know.'

'You do, do you?'

'Used to see them around, right through the district, Mr Hardy and this would be the first Mrs Hardy. Always biking.'

The two men look at Alex's bicycle, as if it was asserting some crucial statement, talking to them.

'I met her only once or twice,' says Mr Cockerell. 'Of course, like many, I loved Thomas Hardy for years before I was fortunate to meet the owner of the name. Originally I came on business to Max Gate in 1911, representing then the Fitzwilliam Museum at Cambridge.' He looks to see whether Alex is writing this down—he isn't. The notebook is gone of course. Alex knows Cockerell's story. 'To assist Mr Hardy in the preservation and distribution of his manuscripts, lodging them in collections of national significance.'

Alex has not taken his eye off the bicycle. 'They were quite a picture, the cyclists. Mr Hardy had a Rover "Cob" and the one time I remember, Mrs Hardy, Mrs Emma Hardy, probably she was in her sixties or more, a determined old bird, fell off and hurt her ankle, broke it I believe, in some pain, and was taken in to the nearest place which was my aunt's house near Talbothays, and cared for and given a glass of water.'

'It seems you have a wonderful story yourself, Peters.'

'But the other part of the story, Mr Cockerell, told as you could imagine with relish by my elderly aunt, should you happen to know the sort, was that Mr Hardy, having seen his wife to the door of that stranger's house, stranger to him, and into some sort of care, announced he would carry on, cycling alone, not wanting to waste the perfect day, as he described it.' Alex gives his ironic smile.

'I must go in now, Peters.'

At the sound of the door shutting the hare leaps into plain sight, then bounces away again.

Mr Cockerell enters, carrying his bag, to find Mrs Florence standing directly in front of him, pale, exhausted, shining.

'My dear,' he says, 'how are you? You look…wonderful.'

'Oh, Sydney, that's absurd. Is he still there? I've forgotten his name.'

'I fought him off. Local paper.'

She stares at him for a moment. Has she forgotten who he is?

Look at her: she has the large sad lacklustre eyes of a childless woman; great docility and readiness, as if she had learnt her part; not great alacrity but resignation, in welcoming more visitors…

Finally she speaks, 'What would we do without you, Sydney? But there should be someone to take your things.

Where's Nellie? Here, let me.' She moves to take his bag but he swings it away from her.

'I'm here, ma'am,' I say. Neither of them looks.

'Now *that* is absurd, Florence. I can take these up myself. And how was the night? How is he?'

She shrugs. 'When is James due, do you know?'

'Later, I think. This evening.'

She nods. 'Yes, that's what he said, I remember now. You missed Kate yesterday, cheered everyone up as per normal. Told us it was pointless to hope.'

'I'm sorry to hear that. I'll settle myself and then, if I may, just pop my head in. I won't wake him if…'

'We await the doctor of course, lots of awaiting at present. Well, I must see where everyone is. It's so quiet. Calm before the storm, do you think, Sydney?'

'We must——.' But he runs out of steam.

'Batten the hatches?' she says.

'I do think we are as well-prepared as we can be.'

Mrs Florence smiles at this. 'So kind of you to make all these visits, Sydney. Please, it's your home too. Though the way things are, that simply seems to mean we ignore you. The servants are as thrown out by all of this as we are. Can you bear it?'

'Ma'am,' I say.

'Please do, please ignore me. There's only one focus, and that's as it should be.'

From outside there's the noise of a bicycle falling which makes Mrs Florence jump a little in the shoulders. 'Who's there?' she says sharply. 'Go, Nellie!'

'Let me see the chap again,' says Mr Cockerell, putting down his bag.

I follow the Cock.

'I'll talk to the luggage then until you return,' she says behind us.

A fox walks through the leaves. In the trees, the spires of Stinsford. Mr Hardy believes in the fox, in its screams at night. A vixen and her cubs. The damp grass noses the fox. It sniffs and passes on its secretive mission. Rabbits hoot in the branches. Claws on the mossy bark. Birdsong from holes, half-covered in sticks, half-drowned. Flying Vs. Calls on the air, all sorts. The moles. Otters in pools, underground. They walk around like snakes with arms, like drowned puppies, like huge drunk rats. He lies under the covers, smaller and smaller, growing whiskers, hair. He crawls into the sheep pen on his hands and knees. Hello, my friends—is this where you suffer? Is this the place?

Our Alice chops parsley in the kitchen. She has a skill with the knife. Mrs Florence has drifted in, has been standing quietly, and suddenly Alice is aware of her.

These people! How strange that we were in this other world, only yesterday. To hear their voices clear as bells still, clear as crystal. They give off a hum. The smell of onions, lard decreasing. Since then, of course, over a lifetime, a lot of things have happened, some painful, some joyous, most of it utterly standard, some of it quite individual I think. For many years, married and a mother, I wouldn't say to anyone that I'd worked at Max Gate. I wouldn't deny it but I wouldn't volunteer it either. No doubt this was the strange pride and secretiveness we feel about having been close to greatness—because I knew he was great, a great writer that is. Definitely he wasn't a great man. I don't mean only that he wasn't 'nice' or generous or thoughtful about others. He wasn't. More than that, I doubt that he was particularly brave. There was a timidity about him, I thought. Did I think it then? Yes, it's likely. Still, we all knew his significance and importance and you could feel this operating as a force around him. In company he used his outward mildness very effectively. Visitors often seemed to crane forward, staring expectantly as if waiting for the real Thomas Hardy to emerge from the shell of this sweet-looking old man. What did he really mean when he asked if they wanted more tea? When he gazed at the terrible little dog, what was he seeing? How much of Hardy was with them that day in the garden? They were certain to feel as if he was hiding inside, a powerful giant asleep in the body of a failing elderly gent. If they didn't feel that, there would be only disappointment to experience. *This* is Thomas Hardy?

Did my secretive pride in having lived alongside such a life also include the vain belief that I knew the nature of his evasive soul, that I'd seen the giant and knew its moves? Surely not. All I knew was how he affected those around him and what we all ended up doing either because of him or despite him. That's what I remember and that's what my 'story' is about. Funny this idea I'm controlling it all. But the controlling person is here as well as everyone else.

I have to listen to her say other things. Such as: another reason I believe I didn't mention Max Gate was the equally self-defeating sense of resentment common to people whose lives are associated with single events, certain periods, as if the span of one's existence came down to a few crucial years. These weren't my crucial years, I wanted to say. Training as a teacher was more important to me, falling in love with Robert in middle-age and marrying him was more important to me, bringing up Jenny was more important. Of these developments, no one from my life at Max Gate knew a thing. This might be one reason why I've never actively talked of the time. Really they all belonged to what I came to regard as my prolonged adolescence. That 'Nellie' wasn't someone I looked back on fondly and the images that came to mind of Max Gate were mostly painful ones. Now I'm curious—am I? I'm old and curious. Who was that person? And the people around her—Florence, Alice, Alex—who were they? What were we all thinking?

At the time there was someone I told.

When my mother used to talk about the past, I could barely listen. It was too boring. I thought her selfish and stuck, and she grew reticent—perhaps hurt by my meanness. Then as I got a little older, with a life of my own to report back on, we had something to share. Perhaps she thought me selfish, as no doubt I was. She never appeared to tire of hearing about life at Max Gate, and slowly it brought out her own stories again, which now made sense to me and were of interest. I granted her the life she'd lived! She'd been a seamstress and then worked for a milliner, before marrying my dairyman father quite late. They'd thought she was unable to conceive until she had me, in her forties. And it turned out I was the same. My father died when I was four.

Alice almost drops the knife. 'Oh! Mrs Florence, gave a scare as a ghost.'

'Mr Cockerell is here.'

'But I didn't hear thic door.' She starts to move towards the door, wiping her hands on her apron.

'He let himself in. Never mind now. What are you doing?'

'Making his broth, ma'am, his kettle-broth. He always asks for it when he's poorly. I should chop his parsley till it most disappears else Mr Hardy will end in having his smile flecked in green with bits in his teeth, as he complained once, but nicely. He was teasing, that's all.'

'Maybe I should take it to him once you're done.'

'Cook never chops up the ingredients as fine so he asked specially I do it. She was displeased and called me his favourite. I never aimed for it. And think he likes Nellie as much as me. Or Miss Eva. He likes her.'

'You're very kind to him, and he appreciates it.'

'Glad of these onions too, ma'am. The way my eyes are, it's a great excuse, for the tears I mean. I'm easy to cry. Would you take it to him, do you think?'

'Oh if you think it a good idea.'

'Only you're a bit unsteady, Mrs Florence.'

She touches her head. 'They've given me things to help me sleep.'

'And I need to do the bacon in his room, like he likes it. A steady hand in the fire. I do it on his bedroom fire. He likes that.'

'I don't function in the fumes.'

'Most go up the chimney.'

'No.'

'If I'm doing the bacon, you could be there with the broth.'

'I'll see him afterwards.'

Alice wipes the blade with her finger and continues to chop. 'Once the broth's given him the strength. Will you read to him again tonight, Mrs Florence?'

'He seems to find something in it. He asked for Browning.'

'I don't know how to cook browning, ma'am.'

'Robert Browning. "Rabbi ben Ezra." "Grow old along with me!/The best is yet to be."'

Alice thinks. What is this raving lunatic on about? 'He is old, that's true.'

Mrs F. idly opens a cupboard and touches a pot. 'Mr Barrie, Sir James, said he thought him more cheerful the other day, and stronger too. We always feel better when he comes. Mr Hardy is very fond of Sir James and thinks of him as something like the divines, angelic a little. And I think we can see that.'

Sir James is no taller than Alice. Are angels short? He bounces on his feet to make himself bigger. We call him the Sprite, sometimes the Dwarf. In isolation he looks pretty and well-formed but put him next to a real man—. It seems clear that Mrs Florence is under his spell. His size makes him seem friendly, even easily managed. Still it struck us as unlikely that the Barrie had anything stirring in the undergrowth for anyone. Was he really just a boy dressed up? Sometimes we'd call him Peter. In addition he was an unlucky person—unlucky if you knew him, fatal in fact. Cook had the stories—of drownings and deaths, all very murky. Like the alkaline douche.

'Miss Kate wasn't so taken, I mean with her brother's position,' says Alice. 'She told me not to blind myself to what is coming.'

'Miss Kate is thinking back on her own father, Mr Hardy's father, and his end, and that colours her view.'

'When is it coming?' says Alice.

'When? We must expect it soon.'

'I hate expecting. When I was a child, I couldn't wait.'

'But that is a stupid thing to say, Alice! Meaning you wish Mr Hardy—'

'No! My word, no! Only it is in my thoughts always and wish it weren't, that moment when…' She puts down the knife and a single choking sob comes up.

'All right. All right. No one is saying the right things, but still we must try. There, there. No need for tears.'

Alice wipes her dry eyes with her apron and picks up the knife.

'Just a few weeks ago the doctor said Mr Hardy has the arteries of a man of sixty and that all his organs are sound.'

Arteries and organs—fuck me, Alice thinks. Or fuck her. Someone please.

Mrs F. is in an odd inspectory mood, looking in a drawer and moving things around. The cutlery shifting gives Alice the creeps. Why won't the woman leave us now? The trouble is she has nothing to do. Imagine having nothing to do!

'What can I do, Alice? How can I help?'

'Nothing to do here, Mrs Florence.'

'It all seems a bit grimy though. Where's Cook?'

'Looking for something in the garden. I'll fix all that once I'm done with the broth.'

'We can't let it all slide, Alice.'

'No, ma'am. And I'm too sorry to have said that thing to make you think that before. Mr Hardy is the soul of Max Gate to its very bones. Cook remembers when Mrs Emma passed away.'

'As I do. What is the relevance?'

'That it caught unawares. And Dolly Gale, who was working back then I think, was sent to his study where he was writing and told him that the mistress was horrible unwell and Mr Hardy carried on a bit writing, not seeming to take it in, and eventual said to Dolly, "Your collar is crooked." He was working very hard on his book. When finally they went up, Mrs Emma was gone.'

F. had come towards her. 'Such a story, Alice, to whom does it do credit?'

'Cook tells it.'

'And you repeat it. For what reason?'

Alice is in tears again, but they are tears of rage and frustration at never being able to say the right thing in Mrs F.'s presence. The two women look at each other in disguised hatred, preparing for something, an embrace perhaps, Alice realises with terror. She sees the other woman hesitating, churning inside at the decision, the move she knows she should make to console the wretched maid. The pain of her conscience is visible on her twisted face. Be that kind person who hugs the servants! Start this now. Soon you will be in sole charge of this house. Make a new beginning. Make a movement forward and hold out your arms and soon it will be over. How I knew

45

this oddness and trembling on boundaries. Of everyone in F.'s life, including most definitely her husband, I believe I had the most physical contact with her. Later Alice tells me it was the knife which saved her. Luckily Alice is still holding the knife and she raises it slightly, looking down again at the chopping board. When she glances up again, F. is glum, resigned to what she believes is her own coldness and failure but is only the distortion of impulses she shares with—with us. This makes Alice feel a small prick of pity. Somehow she can't hate her though she finds her physically ugly, those deep rings under her eyes, the sour shape of her mouth, the dowdy cardigans, the cover-up black cloche hats. The failure to convert available funds into anything approaching style drives Alice, who has a good fashion eye, insane. The sprigged voile dress, the black shoes, that rapist's necklace, one twist and you'd buckle at the knees.

Married to a corpse and swooning over a bronchial eunuch.

Alice tidies a pile of the parsley using the back of her blade. 'When I do the bacon on the fire, ma'am, I could open the window a bit, do you think?'

'Open the window?' says Mrs Florence.

'A tiny bit.'

'But you can't! It's winter. It's snowing!'

'It was the fumes I was thinking about, ma'am, and your functions on account of them. That ye could share the meal with us.'

'Alice, are you clear on this? I will not be there for Mr Hardy's supper, and so my reactions to the bacon are irrelevant. Most of the fumes will go up the chimney, the rest will give Mr Hardy that nostalgic pleasure he's spoken of with you. Maybe his mother burnt bacon once. His sentimentality is world-renowned. I doubt he will eat the bacon.'

'No.'

'Pick at it is the most he will do, as both of us know. Probably, Alice, if you forgot the bacon he wouldn't mind at all, wouldn't notice.'

'Then what is the point of doing it at all!' This time Alice won't cry. She will not melt. She will be thic blade.

There's barking again.

F. rests her fingers on the necklace. Familiar gesture. It means: now watch as I dredge up a moral lesson of great fineness and utter unreality. 'Listen,' says Mrs Florence, 'he's a very old man. Very old. Having lived a great life. Having lived to be admired by all. It's not given to many to see the fruits of their labours realised in this world. Mr Hardy is a lucky man. With great achievements right in view. He leaves us then, he prepares to do so, with some satisfaction in his life's work. That's our consolation and his. And we should allow that sheen to settle on our sadness, and to brighten it, if only a jot. One of the great men, one of the greatest, of English Letters.'

'But a simple soul too, ma'am, if I may. Of us, if I may. My mother was born at Bockhampton same as Mr Hardy, before snatched to Somerset.'

'Yes, I remember, at the interview when you came to us, the connection delighted Mr Hardy.'

'He asked all about her. She's never much settled in Somerset.'

F. walks to the window. 'When is Dr Mann here? I need him here.' She sounds soft and absent once more. Is it an act? Alice often thinks this: they're acting! They've heard of emotions and know what they look like, and this is what they look like: a woman leans her head against the window of her own house, a house which will soon be hers alone, hers to do whatever she wants with, a house of male callers and sympathy and help and whatever she wishes it to be full of—and this is the woman whose unhappiness we should all gather around and minister to and believe in. But Alice didn't. Not at this moment. She simply wanted to be left alone to get on with her boring jobs.

Anyway, Alice doesn't tell the next story from any impulse to draw the older woman back, or even to punish her. She wants her gone certainly but she's speaking now, she realises, for herself and for her mother, whom she misses with a sudden sharpness. 'Mr Hardy liked to think back to Bockhampton,' she says. 'I remember when another gentleman with his little daughter came down, it was the Murrys, and the girl was sat on Mr Hardy's knee, and he took out his handkerchief and said to her, do I think something might be made of this? Asking himself, I mean. But only if he could remember how it goes, which he said he couldn't. He looked and looked at the handkerchief. Then we watched as his fingers remembered what his mind was unable to. Was as if he was watching himself in the act. And he made a rabbit! From just the handkerchief and cried, Oh look, here he is, the rabbit! Surprised himself. As if hadn't done it but someone else, some spirit. It was from his own childhood, he said. He had tears.'

F. continues to talk to the window. 'What they give me to sleep wakes me, but in the most vile foliage so it's shapes

I see, animals, and nothing calms and nothing holds. Alice, are we to be walled in by trees forever? Trees! I sometimes wonder whether his gloomy outlook was hatched by having so many trees in his line of vision. Austrian pines, planted to keep things out—the wind, prying eyes. Where is Dr Mann?'

Alice keeps chopping. The pieces are getting tiny, coating the blade.

'She once told me the most ludicrous thing,' says Mrs Florence, addressing the window still. 'She made up such nonsense. It was that Tom thought the reason some of the trees he planted failed to develop was that he'd looked at them before breakfast on an empty stomach. And she told me this with a straight face. How absurd she was, huffy, rambling, inconsequent, full of suspicions and jealousies and affronts. But now...well, who knows.'

Chopping, Alice tells me, is her favourite thing. With a sharp knife, I suppose, one can deal to things with a sort of secret power, making what looms larger and larger, smaller and sometimes unrecognisable.

At the same time, we are with Alex and his bicycle at the gate. He and I do not make any acknowledgement, a fact that to anyone half-observant would be meaningful. His nose is red from the cold, a detail I'm meanly glad to see since it makes Alex look a bit silly. We haven't spoken since the day I saw him in town with a woman who wasn't me, and I walked up to them, as if under a drug, and said words that really felt as if they were attached to a piece of string and I was some magician making an impossible length of choking material emerge from my mouth. Silk.

A gagging sort of silk. The pair of them could only stare at me and at this performance. It felt as if I'd shamed myself in an irretrievably public way. But theirs was the shame and the display! Yet they looked on with—someone was disappearing in front of their eyes into a vaudevillian character. It wasn't, I suppose, as if I'd established a claim on him. We weren't engaged, had never mentioned the future, a future. Indeed were drawn to each other, as much on my side as his, by this unspoken pact of carefreeness and the deferment of plans. I was still young and had the feeling I needed to remain so. But what are your plans, people asked me—and I said none, I have none! On the street, bawling at that pair, I was surprised to understand an idea of the future had been there, perhaps all along. Anyway, Mr Cockerell is too distracted, too cold to notice much, or more likely utterly uninterested in whatever is passing between me and Alex.

By now I'm used to the bitterness of the air, the carpet beating having got the blood going. Besides, I remember thinking, but it's not the outside temperature, it's you, you're chilled. They talk about bicycles again.

'As I remember,' says Mr Cockerell, 'Tom once said that cycling you can go out a long distance without coming into contact with another mind, not even a horse's, and therefore without dissipating any little mental energy that has arisen in the course of the morning's application. It seems a kind of motto, Peters. Good day once more.' The Cock walks again towards the gate under the tunnel of privet hedge and I turn to follow.

Alex rests his bicycle against his side and writes in his notebook. 'Thank you for the quote, Mr Cockerell. "Not even a horse's mind." Very good! I enjoy the solitude myself. And I don't blame Mr Hardy at all for abandoning his upset wife with my aunt. It suggests, as your quote underlines, a sense of purpose not easily swayed.'

The Cock pauses. 'Perhaps the foremost requirement for not only a cyclist but also an author.' He turns. 'But you know he never abandoned her—his Emma. Loved her best when she was gone perhaps. There are the famous poems, Peters, of such passion and attention, addressed not to the present Mrs Hardy but to the departed one. Off the record, the publication and critical success of those works is near the source of Florence's troubles. Off the record, I say again.'

'Off the record, how so, sir? Jealousy?'

Cockerell looks at me for the first time, though not as anyone in particular; I'm a stand-in. He appears to weigh whether he can pursue the point. 'A kind of outrage, I imagine. To be thirty-five years old, just married to a septuagenarian, and outdone by one's predecessor.' I've been weighed as nothing. Or perhaps this is the proof that the master is effectively if not actually gone—Mr Cockerell can speak as if there are no consequences. It occurs to me too that he is engaged with Alex because it is preferable to being inside with Mrs Florence. Being so lovely together, it took time to see how they hated each other. 'Especially as the predecessor, when alive, did not exactly act as soulmate. Emma faded early. Remember, Florence was part of this household, as secretary to Mr Hardy, long before Emma's death. By which stage all her illusions regarding Emma were gone. She'd observed many a holy row.'

Suddenly Alex begins to recite. I almost gasp at the

unfairness of this. I can't believe it. The poems are ours. Our code, I'd thought. Shocked as he pretended to be that I'd never read the poems of the man in whose house I lived and worked, Alex had taken it on himself to fix that. Now he doesn't care that anyone receives them, even Cockerell, whom he knows cannot be trusted. Unless—. Unless he's making love to Cockerell. And doing it in front of me. I feel chilled again, abandoned all over again.

'And to me, though Time's unflinching rigour
In mindless rote, has ruled from sight
The substance now, one phantom figure
Remains on the slope, as when that night
Saw us alight.
I look and see it there, shrinking, shrinking,
I look back at it amid the rain
For the very last time; for my sand is sinking,
And I shall traverse old love's domain
Never again.'

Something I forgot until now: Alex had acted on the stage. He'd been in one of the local productions of Hardy. He may have had ambitions but I can't remember for sure. His voice was strong, not too hammy. Clearly he'd developed a good memory.

The Cock, amazingly, is worked upon. 'I see some genuine attachment there, Peters.'

I laugh without meaning to—bitterly. Both men appear too far inside the game to register any criticism.

'I hope ye don't doubt it, Mr Cockerell. I know a few of them by heart. And when I say them, they bring to mind someone of my own I lost—my only sister, with whom I fought often. Regret may be a useless emotion but that can't dim its power.'

Sister? She's new. Mr Cockerell mumbles something about the significance of sisters and then says, 'When will the man from the *Times* be in the village, do you think?'

'Is he coming, sir? What should I tell him?'

'What should you tell the man you haven't seen? You're a mysterious chap, Mr Peters.'

'We're looking into the greatest mystery here, I think, Mr Cockerell.'

'I phoned the *Times* yesterday, just to be on the alert.'

'All right,' says Alex.

The Cock blows a cloud of breath above him and looks again at the house. 'Two years ago, Florence had a tumour removed successfully from her neck. Word was she named the tumour "Emma". I'm unsure how I come to say all this to you, Peters. I might credit your skill as journalist in prompting me, or the circumstances here. Needless to say only a few early parts of our conversation should be…' Suddenly he grips my arm. 'You! You, my dear, shall be our witness.'

'Witness?' I say.

'As to what is on the record and off.'

'I've only half been listening, sir.'

'Which half?' Cockerell still has my arm. He smells of talcum powder.

'No need to include the girl,' says Alex. 'It's all perfectly understood, Mr Cockerell. I recall now that the man from the *Times* has a booking at the local hotel where my cousin works.'

He releases me. 'You're an immensely well-connected man, Peters.'

'Oh we're all connected here, Mr Cockerell. Round here we all die famous. Is Sir James Barrie also inside, sir?'

'He is not. Now really we are both getting very cold. This poor girl won't thank us.'

Alex turns to me and speaks as if he's been saving me up. 'Miss Nellie Titterington, how is everyone in the house coping?' His look is blandly sympathetic, with just a hint of wryness aimed, I think, directly into the heart of what's absurd in standing here with Cockerell, romancing him while I watch.

I have to bite down to stop from laughing in his face or striking him.

Cockerell raises one hand. 'Getting this girl into trouble will help no one.'

'Quite right, quite right. But one final question of you sir, if I may? And forgive my prematurity in asking. But last week I came up by way of the family plot at Stinsford churchyard, at St Michael's, which no doubt accounts for Mrs Emma Hardy being in my mind since her name is there on the headstone and space for Thomas to lie with her, among the forebears. His parents and grandparents, and a sister. I believe Kate has also been in the house, another sister. A beautiful spot it is, in the churchyard, and the great fittingness of it for the figure who, as I said, named us in the world's eyes more permanently than my father named me or his father him. You'd be aware of the place, at Stinsford, both restful and yet involved in the drama of mood and season which grips us all. You're from London perhaps, Mr Cockerell? And there I also met Reverend Cowley, the vicar of Stinsford.'

Cockerell answers coolly: 'Yes, I know of Cowley.'

'To imagine Thomas Hardy eternally there among us was, I don't mind saying, briefly the cause of an utter loss of journalistic objectivity. I wept to think of his name chiselled and weathering, and to think of his bones in our soil, becoming our earth. You'll consider me one of his own characters soon, Mr Cockerell, stepped from a novel, and maybe this—' Alex reached for my arm with his splayed fingers and rested there, '—is Tess! Ha!'

Here Cockerell also said 'Ha' but less convincingly. Perhaps he wasn't sure my name wasn't Tess. I removed my arm from Alex's grip. It was amazing to be in the middle of this, two men putting on such a show and for whom? I wanted to think partly it was for me but that would have made it more routine, more expected than it was. Can two men be with a woman and not be in this sort of fight? How boring. Yet there was another man present too—Mr Hardy himself. Three men. The tussle was in expertise and depth of knowledge. Alex was probably winning on all fronts except that of personal intimacy. For the first time I saw Stanley Cockerell's intellectual vulnerability and it surprised me. It may have even surprised Alex and encouraged him along the path he eventually took, where he finally overreached.

'But anyway,' says Alex, 'it gave me the same shiver that goes through my body on our ancient roads when I turn up by the wheel of my bicycle an image of one of the Caesars that was currency for some inhabitant who walked these same paths that sound our steps and these same grasses that tickle our shins before Christ came. I have a small collection of old coins.'

'Truly? I collect things myself. Paintings, pots. I was for several years assistant and advisor to William Morris, the designer.'

'Seems you collect people as well, Mr Cockerell. Still, I had a feel, a shock as something electric, which was, I suppose, history, running through my being at Stinsford churchyard.'

Somehow I was moved to speak. 'When they dug the foundations of Max Gate,' I say, 'they found two Roman burial places.' There were things under glass in the Hardy Museum: fragments of a cup, chips of bone—copies, the real items taken to a real museum.

For Cockerell my information is obvious, known. 'What was your question, Peters?'

'Has thought yet been given to the service, his laying to rest?'

Cockerell, agitated, looks back at the house where a curtain moves, concealing a figure. 'As you yourself said, that's premature. But bear in mind his importance to the whole of England and, as our conversation seems to have returned to this same point, not only this small, charming parcel of the country.'

'He won't go the Abbey, sir, will he?'

'I didn't mention it. Did Reverend Cowley?'

'Rumour's round. I said to them spreading it, that won't happen. Not Tom on his "Cob" Rover! As a boy, I saw him once out riding with another gentleman, also a visitor from London, turned out to be Rudyard Kipling. The very one, in cycling knickerbockers. Both on bicycles. He was riding very poorly, Kipling was. Very poorly indeed. Stiffly and ungainly. Some years ago. On the occasion he was looking to buy land here Kipling was, somewhere out by Weymouth, but never did. Returned from where he came, and Mr Hardy back to his house here. Back to Max Gate. Ye see the tracks along the ground, where the bicycles have made their marks.'

The three of us look down at the hard ground, its puddles of snow.

'And I move along them to attend to our friend.'

'Attached with our blessings and prayers, Mr Cockerell, as you go. Fastened tight with those. Good day. Good day, Nellie.'

I open the door and the Cock goes inside. 'Strange chap,' he murmurs. Then he draws a deep breath and twice he claps together his gloved hands as if in achievement. 'My God,' he tells the hallway, 'there are great smells in this house. I'm absolutely starving!'

It's not night at Max Gate but I think of night. As if the day has rotated already. But it hasn't. Of course it's because you're in bed. At night all the creatures walk. The birds with round eyes, the sleek-headed things that can swim. Bats, blind animals, and the ones who catch them unawares. Foxes sitting like children in the branches so they can swoop down on ropes. The rusty teeth of buried traps, furry legs. Mice. Badgers and fish breathing in the leaves. Pigs that are wild and spiky. Tiny trails of blood on the stalks of grass. Toadstools. Lichen. Something croodling, a culver or cutty. Frightened fowl, lost.

A cattle-truck passes the house, moaning.

The light from Alex's bicycle picks out the eyes of things sitting in the grass. His gun.

The doctor sat in the kitchen, eating up the broth, his narrow back to the fire. His bald head and the back of the spoon that he turns over to lick once he's finished the bowl, they both shine in a way we don't care for. Nor does Cook enjoy him taking his food down here, though he says it'll be less fuss and work for everyone. Mrs Florence isn't to know of course.

The best fire in the house is right here in the kitchen and Cook keeps it burning to slightly torment Mr Hardy, who's a rare visitor—even rarer in the last few weeks. He's been known to wonder aloud about the expense involved. Would the work not be keeping them all warm enough?

Now the doctor wants to talk to us, without Mrs Florence. A few practical matters.

'Who is shaving him?' he asks. 'I understand there's no man-servant?'

'Not for years, sir,' says Cook. 'Does it himself, Doctor, always has.'

'That can't happen any longer, I'm afraid,' he says.

Alice starts to sob but she stops once the doctor looks at her. She can switch on and off just like that.

'Has anyone any experience in this?'

Alice and Cook shake their heads. They both reach to take his bowl and spoon, to have something in their hands, a job at the sink.

'What about Bert?' Alice blurts. 'Mr Stephens?'

'Stephens? The gardener?' says the doctor.

'Don't be stupid, girl,' says Cook.

'You think he's a plant or bush? Get at the job with his clippers?' The doctor laughs. 'What about you, Nellie?'

Our grandfather had lost the power of his hands and we watched our mother do him. How to remember to catch the soap in his ears since it dried unpleasantly. 'No, sir.'

'Well,' says the doctor, rubbing his own chin, which is smooth, 'maybe we won't have to worry about that.'

At the sink, Alice chokes. Cook pats her hand, lightly pinching it too.

Later in the afternoon, after the laundry and luncheon, I'm sent to buy more meat. The rain has finally stopped but the wind is against me going in and the cycling is hard. Nor do the mud-flaps give much protection. The backs of my tights are quickly soaked by the precise line of spray from the tyres, almost as neat as a seam. All told, however, I like the bicycle. And I like it not exactly in the way Mr Hardy spoke of. He didn't want to be interrupted; I do. Pedalling hard, I always feel something is happening. But what? I'm leaving Max Gate, yes. I'm free of Mrs Florence and Cook, certainly. But I'm along the road of possibility. I know each corner, each hateful (upside) and lovely (downside) hill, but I also don't know what will become of me. Most likely nothing. Still, the bicycle is a hopeful creature, dependent on my energy for the most part, and it will reward me if I give myself to it, and I do. Often I'm out of the seat and walking the pedals with all my weight and singing or shouting it is more honestly: 'The teaties be out in knap! The teaties be out in knap!'

I take the opportunity to pick up some sausages for my mother and bring them around to her cottage in Orchard Street. We sit in the kitchen by the gas fire and she tells me I don't look well. I tell her that cycling three miles in the snow probably hasn't done wonders for my energy levels. Still it's a long-running theme that she, with her arthritis, bad knee, gastric problems and failing eyesight, is always 'fine' and I, her robust, strong daughter with the calves of a weightlifter and the arms of a boxer, am poorly. Yet she has only to say it and I feel it, if only slightly. The gas fire is wilting and fumey and I've slumped I know. Her concern chips at my confidence. Maybe I'm not as healthy as all that. I feel tired. You're pale, she says, bringing the teapot to the table. We talk about Max Gate. She is extremely proud that I have a position in such a house and she's insatiable in her appetite for the gossip. She likes to hear what they eat, what times they are in bed, any changes in the routines. Often she brings up the time at Christmas when Mr Hardy fed Wessex goose and plum pudding until the dog literally fell over, moaning with pain. Finally I was asked to bring the empty cake trolley and we placed the dog on top of it and I wheeled him out. Also she enjoys my complaining about Cook.

She makes more tea—it's what she lives on, and then to my questions about the house, the winter, she waves a hand, no, no, let's not be bothered with that stuff.

'Will you see your chap?' she asks in a lull.

'I won't.'

'What, have ye had a fight?'

'Leaps to conclusions, doesn't she,' I say, attempting to make it a joke.

But my mother is on a scent. 'There's no tiff can't be mended if there's gentleness on one side.'

'Just the one side then? Not sure if he's the gentle sort, Ma.' She's met and liked Alex and immediately I regret the opening I've given her. Alex was charming with her, talked about her garden. He knows plants.

'Seemed exactly that to me but then maybe it was a front he put on, was it.'

'It's not a subject I'm too fussed to follow up.'

'Oh,' she says.

I've spoken too harshly. Woundedly she turns the cup on her saucer, aligning the patterns. 'Anyway,' I say, more softly, 'poor Mr Hardy is looking very bad.'

She doesn't look up. 'He's rallied before. I wouldn't put it past him to rise again.'

This makes me laugh it's delivered so sulkily. Ma laughs too, a short exhausted noise. She shares the town's impatience with the Hardy story. Two years ago, when he didn't eat his Christmas pudding, nor listen to the New Year's bells on the radio, we'd expected something that didn't happen. False alarms have been added to the historical testiness.

'Dearie,' she says, 'I'm sure you know what's best with the chap. I'm only saying don't be proud. I know where the pride comes from and what havoc it can wreak.'

'Havoc! What an exciting time you imagine I'm having, Ma.'

'You're tilty today.'

'And you're timmersome.'

She stands to clear the cups away, visibly wincing but she won't let me help. She tells me I have enough running around after them up at the House. Here I can sit and do sweet nothing. It's only a few minutes out of the day.

She leads me to the bedroom to show me some material she bought recently. She'll make an apron and something else for the young mother across the road. The woman's husband was killed a year ago in an accident and she is mad for a man—the husband's best friend—who for whatever reason won't commit to her even though there've been many signs from him that he'd like to. Another woman, without children, is also after him. I've heard about this situation many times. My mother lives it and the widow confides in her. I admire the material for the apron and say I should be getting back to Max Gate but Ma hasn't finished.

'When I was very young I remember a scandal. Three local girls had been practising spells, an old old spell designed to win someone's love. We were talking about it the other day.'

'Were you?'

'Yes. They'd killed a pigeon and cut its heart into three pieces.'

'Oh lovely,' I say.

'Then they'd left the pieces on the doorstep of the intended one. Were all three in love with him? Can't remember. Anyway, that night one of the girls became very ill, with a fever or something it seemed like. And she told her worried mother that she must go to the house of the intended, the victim, and say these words to the mother of that house, "Do ye come along and see my poor child, she is so ill I don't like to bide with her alone!" If she did this, everything would be right again. But then it came out, because the mother of the girl could see at once her daughter wasn't ill after all, that there was some game or mischief. They traced it back and the girls confessed. It was a scandal at the time and I've never forgotten the words "I don't like to bide with her alone".'

'Why a pigeon?' I say.

Ma speaks solemnly. 'Spells only work with the exact right thing.'

I can't help but laugh again. Which is also wrong. 'Were they punished?'

'How do I know? I'm sure they were. But they weren't hanged as witches, if that's what you mean.' She's irritated with me for some reason, though she's never been very superstitious.

'That's a relief.'

When she kissed me at the door, she was still not fully back from her story, the three girls and the pigeon heart. She was distant, wary, disappointed even—in me perhaps, or was that too self-regarding? I was only one part of her life. A child should remember that. She may have just been thinking about her young widow's problems. And I was thinking, who is this person to occupy my mother's mind—thinking it with envy, I suppose. One time she'd used the word 'goodnow' for 'neighbour' when speaking to the widow. Which gave me a shock. Old words were ours, for family. Whenever she spoke of her I had the sense she was saying that somehow these were the details and involvements that you deny me even though you are my daughter. Did I deny her? I told her lots. That the master's favourite lunch was a cup of soup, followed by two boiled eggs, then Dorset knobs and Stilton cheese.

That Lawrence of Arabia was the only man, apart from Mr Hardy of course, with whom Wessex put himself in a subservient position; everyone else, he terrorised.

Riding back to the house, I had the odd feeling of being watched and I couldn't shake a sort of alertness—I was convinced I'd miss something if I let my attention wander for even a second. But what? A calamity obviously, since I was cycling so cautiously, the wool of my scarf stuck to my mouth, shoulders tensed. The road was empty all the way.

The ice in its saucer, a thin crust of milk underneath. The hard shins on the man. The cat looks up from the white crystals, sparkling. Two elderly figures are coming up the path: a woman and a man. In the cat's mind these are ghosts. It's Kate and Henry Hardy. They have their arms linked. The cat is gone from its spot. The pair stop on the path, looking up at their breath, taking a moment. These are their graves. Mother and Father, others. Tom's first and beside her, his place. Their places, lined with evergreens and in spring yellow and bronze chrysanthemums under the shelter of the great yew tree. Birds lift off, settling on headstones further away. There are flowers made of stone, in places eaten by the wind, the snow. Bleating, purring. One time their father threw a rock and killed a fieldfare right in front of Tom. They walk on towards the markers, up the slippery path. He repeated that often, that Father had done it and not thought a thing of it but carried on his way, the animal's life gone, judged as nothing.

At four o'clock there's a delivery by taxi of several bunches of grapes—wonderful bunches—from Mr Newman Flower. Having shown them first to Mrs Florence, I take them to Mr Hardy's door where my knock is answered by Miss Eva. She accepts them in silence, bowing slightly, and closes the door.

'Listen to this, Nellie.' Mrs Florence sits at the little desk in her room, reading aloud from a thick stack of pages. She flicks through them, choosing passages at random, almost angrily, though she started calmly enough. She's summoned me to work on fixing the hem of a coat I doubt she'll wear again, and which job is better suited to Alice, but she wants me here and this is the pretext.

We've already laughed over a description she's read out of Mr Hardy falling off his bicycle on a trip to Bristol many years ago. He came off in the mud and was rubbed down by a kindly coal-heaver with one of his sacks. F. laughed and I followed her lead; it wasn't entirely clear from the beginning that the incident was supposed to be funny. How would the coal-sack be clean, I was wondering. Plus there's a note of hysteria in F.'s manner. Either the readings are designed to release the strain she's under or they're yet another signal she won't be released.

It's dark already though the curtains aren't closed yet. Dry snow soundlessly strikes the window and bounces off, some of it mounting on the sill like ash. There's the feeling of being slowly buried, of airlessness, and I've found myself pulling at the top button of my blouse. F. looks red in the face. Along the hall her sister sits by T. H.'s bed.

Eva is like Florence only more so—more self-denying. Yet somehow this works in Eva to generate not the waves of unhappiness that come from her older sister but a satisfied purpose that begins to look like peacefulness, as if setting the bar so low for personal achievement, any day in which she doesn't draw attention to herself is a victory. (It's hard not to seem satirical about such a figure when summoning her. This isn't how I felt.) Always alert to others' distress, Eva has managed to eliminate any suggestion of solicitousness. She is not the sort of kindly female one wishes to kick, and though there was little to respond to in her person, I find myself liking her. She is as mild with us as with them, which can be a shock still; Alice doesn't like it much since she, Alice, still relies on being bullied to guide her as to what she should be doing at any given moment. Eva is also an excellent nurse, though I don't think that follows from her qualities. She doesn't grind Mr Hardy down with her unflappable, unobtrusive manner. He does seem to like her genuinely and submits to her. Despite the situation, the sisters weren't close and didn't become closer. Eva was, thinking about it now, probably also being paid.

'There's a brass tablet in the church at Stinsford—perhaps you've seen it,' says Mrs Florence. 'The tablet commemorates the connection of Mr Hardy's grandfather and father with the church. They used to provide music for various services. And Mr Hardy played there as a boy, accompanying them. He played the violin. And the tablet was put there in 1902.'

'Year of my birth, ma'am,' I say.

'Very good!' she says. 'The inscription was written by Mr Hardy and he wrote it in Latin, you see.'

'I'm afraid I don't know the language, ma'am.'

'The reason he wrote it in Latin was this. He believed that English was changing so rapidly that if he wrote it in English, future generations wouldn't be able to read it.'

'I see.'

She slaps the pages lightly with her palm. 'You see? Future generations. So he made it foolproof for the ages, for eternity!' The hysterical note breaks through, throwing her voice higher and louder than normal.

'Hoping there'd be Latin in eternity,' I say.

'Yes! The contributions of the Hardys to this little church—they played violins passably, I think—would be recognised by whoever came after us, even if the English race, the entire English language had been lost!' She laughs, her mockery clear. She looks savage, exultant. The revelation of naked feeling doesn't mean I've attained some special position; I have the impression she's forgotten I'm in the room listening. These are the thoughts she's been having in private for a long time, years even. Versions have reared up before.

I ask her what it is she's reading from, what all those pages are. She takes a second to understand the question, that I'm here. His life story, she says. His biography. She's been writing his biography these past few years. '"Writing" isn't right,' she says. 'Tom hands me pages of manuscript to type in triplicate, and then we go over these and he produces revisions in the margins and I re-type everything and we check them again. It's his work, his life story, but it's in the third person, "He did this, he did that", so it appears Tom hasn't been involved at all.'

I don't understand what this means and F. tells me not to mind. She flips the pages again and reads aloud, sometimes with obvious sarcasm, at other times earnestly, as if she can't settle on her own attitude to the material.

'There was a bed in the family that had originally belonged to Tom's great-grandfather on his mother's side.' She stops. 'On his mother's side of the bed. Ha.' Back to the reading. 'It was a huge black poster bed decorated with the Twelve Apostles. Over time the Apostles came loose and Tom remembers playing with these figures as dolls.' She rests her hand on the page and looks up at the wall. Then she's reading again. 'As a boy Tom sometimes was asked by the dairy-maids to write love letters on their behalf, often to men posted abroad as soldiers. He had little understanding of the contents of these letters and the dairy-maids would have had little ability to check that what he wrote was in accord with their dictated feelings. The sweethearts were often living in India or the East Indies. He recalls that one time he followed a goose around for hours until he managed to extract a quill with which to write these letters.'

'A goose,' I say.

'A quill! You see how far back he goes!'

I'm thinking of the goose, how to pull a feather out, though maybe he was waiting for it to shed one. Yes, young Tom wouldn't have caused the bird any pain.

'The Close of Salisbury under a full summer moon on

a windless night,' she reads on. Stops again. Turns pages. Reads: 'We enter Church and we have to say "We have erred and strayed from Thy ways like lost sheep" when what we want to say is "Why are we made to err and stray like lost sheep?" You see?' This last bit seems aimed at me. However, there's no time to answer. '"Why" is the question,' she says gloomily. 'Why why why.' Her head drops back into the page as she mutters to herself. Reads: '"He liked it that the inventor was unknown." Ah, yes this is Gloucester Cathedral, the greatest English contribution to Gothic architecture. "He liked it that the inventor was unknown, like the author of so many noble songs and ballads." Unknown!' Pause, wild staring around the room, as if she's trying to locate the source of an unpleasant noise. Somewhere downstairs a door closes. Reading: 'Half my time—particularly when writing verse—I "believe"— he says "I 'believe'" with quotation marks—"I 'believe'"— hedging his bets, I'd say—he believes in that way he wants immediately to retract if someone calls him on it, thinks him foolish, he believes in spectres, mysteries, voices, intuitions, omens, dreams, haunted places. Haunted places. He believes in haunted places.'

She looks at me fully for the first time, terrified, and I don't know what to say so I tell her something about the coat, that I've almost finished it. How badly I'd made the repair, I see then. She's not interested. She says, 'Do you know, Nellie, that Sir James once asked Mr Hardy to go with him to France.'

'On holiday, ma'am?'

'This was during the war, certainly not a holiday. It was 1917. He asked him to go behind the lines. Sir James was rather desperate. He wanted to visit the grave of a friend.'

'Dangerous?'

'Yes. He asked Tom and Tom said no, he wouldn't go. He was too old.'

'He would have been too.'

This fact annoys her. 'So Sir James went by himself and found the grave of his friend. It was amazingly brave of him. Thousands of graves, near Ypres it was. But he found where his friend was. Amid the carnage, the awful carnage. It was terribly dangerous.'

'Too dangerous for Mr Hardy.'

'Obviously.' She sounds dismissive.

'Mr Hardy's health might have added danger to such a mission,' I say. 'He would have been worried about slowing Sir James down or putting him in awkward positions just by being there, if he'd been unable to proceed as quickly as the younger man.'

She looks puzzled for an instant. I recognise the look. She's considering whether she's been too disloyal to her husband. How is it that her maid is now reassuring her about Thomas Hardy's qualities as a man? And more than that, how does the maid know I'm in love with James? But I am not in love with James, she decides. Or he is the dear friend one loves because it's a simpler love, free of the dailiness that rubs raw the deeper kind between me and Tom.

She studies me, walking over and inspecting my work on the coat. 'Wouldn't Alice be better at that?' she says.

'Yes, ma'am.'

'Then give it to her. I don't know why you're fussing with it.'

I stand up to go as she moves back to the desk and the papers.

'The grapes were a great hit,' she says. It's her peace offering.

'They looked very good.'

'Oh, Nellie, he was like a little boy about them. He offered them to me and to Eva. Very gaily, he wanted the doctor to see them and explained who they were from. He had a few himself. "I'm going on with these!" he told me when I was leaving the room.'

'A great sign he was eating again, ma'am.'

'I did think, walking out, those grapes could be the last thing that give him real pleasure.'

It seems such a sensible statement my objection to it dies in my mouth.

She nods at this non-response. Good. 'You must understand one thing, Nellie. Jealousy of each other in their work is woman's greatest weakness.'

Does she mean me and Alice? Me and her? She and Emma? Something else.

'Because,' she says, 'women are the meanest of created things. And they are only strong when they recognise their weakness and dependence on men.' She turns away from me. 'When he dies, after a time, the book will come out under my name. It will be the first biography. We will have got in first, ahead of the others who will no doubt then begin the process of fabulating and spreading lies and trying to bring him down. But we will have established some things here. We will have told them the truth about the Twelve Apostles bed and the goose with the feather and the swooning illiterate milkmaids!' She laughs sourly.

'They will know that he considered Salisbury the most magical place of all! And they will have it confirmed that graveyards are wonderfully invigorating spots to take one's young wife, especially if they contain the last resting place of one's old wife. God help us!' At this, Mrs Florence puts her head down and starts to cry. It's not fluid but staccato, in the style, as later I'd discover, some men cry, resenting the process, hurt by the surprise of it, unwillingly. (Robert when his mother died; remembering finding him in the bathroom.) These are so unlike Alice's tears or my own that for a second I don't realise she's weeping. But she is weeping.

Two things I feel at the same time: the staggering and theatrical selfishness; and the gut-hurting pain of her loneliness. I find now I dislike her for being in love with the dwarf Barrie. Hard to see him in France being brave. Yet she's right to think of Hardy as cruel and vain and stifling. It's paralysing to try to comprehend her position. But then again, what is she expecting from me? That I rush to console her? That I touch her? Our touches have always been along official lines: smoothing her scalp when brushing her hair, applying cream to the backs of her hands, inadvertent contact with her shoulder or leg when helping her put on items of clothing.

The general agreement was that such touching wasn't really touching. But of course it was, both of us being humans—even me, even her.

What sort of bone-deep effort did it take for that woman to lift her head again, rub her face and smile at me? Remarkably, she did it, though her eyes were glassy and her skin across her neck raw and red. 'If you could take the coat to Alice,' she says, 'that would be much appreciated. Thank you.'

We do our best to keep the place warm. We carry in the wood and coal, rub a thick grease into the window joints. (Not sure if they are/were called joints—think of checking with Robert later. No, that won't work.) There is always water boiling. Mrs Florence upstairs has drunk her cloudy potion.

Mr Cockerell was sitting that night close by the open fire in the living room, flicking through the pages of a book he wasn't reading, and sipping at his glass. I'd attended to the fire. Into the poker, unobserved, I'd inserted the device via which these sounds and images are created in my mind. Here they come.

The Cock puts down the book as the Barrie and Dr Mann enter.

'Barrie!' They shake hands. 'What news, Doctor?'

'Good evening, Mr Cockerell. He's weaker.'

'But he acknowledged you both?'

'There's some confusion but also lucidity.'

Mr Cockerell offers drinks but the doctor tells him he must see Mrs Florence and then be on his way. He pours one for Barrie. 'Florence didn't come down for dinner. She keeps to her room a lot, so she can be close to him, I suppose.'

Barrie gives his drink a little swirl. 'Brave Florence, brave girl.'

'Kate was in again yesterday,' says Cockerell, 'and not much help, I think. Doesn't rate his chances and said so.'

'I'm happy that the fluid at the base of his lungs isn't present now. I feared the recumbent position would increase the chances of hypostatic pneumonia. That particular danger has been averted.'

'Excellent!' says Cockerell. 'His sister is a very gloomy soul.'

'I sometimes think the family carries the melancholy Tom extinguishes by writing,' says Barrie.

'The heart, though, is still very weak.' Dr Mann takes two pieces of paper from his pocket and gives them to Cockerell. 'Mrs Hardy gave me these, to pass on. They are his, dictated not an hour or more ago.'

'Good Lord, he won't stop.'

'Poems?' says Barrie.

'Of a sort,' says Cockerell.

Dr Mann had moved across to the bookshelves and was looking at titles. 'Mr Hardy said a strange thing but characteristic perhaps. We were not in the vicinity of the subject. He said that his own views on life were so extreme that he did not usually state them.'

'Characteristic indeed, Doctor,' says Cockerell. 'Tom's been attacked for his philosophy too often not to be wary now, even now.'

'The basis of the attacks?'

'Bleakness, pessimism.'

'He prefers the term "meliorist",' says Barrie. 'He wants things better.'

'But sees that they are not, which I've always thought a sensible position.'

'"Whether the human and kindred animal races survive till the exhaustion or destruction of the globe…pain to all upon it, tongued or dumb, shall be kept down to a minimum by loving kindness." Loving kindness, Doctor. That's his idea.'

'I've known him as a patient only, and as a gentle old man, quite cheery, now perhaps as a friend too, with a mutual interest in history I've discovered. But I'm hardly a reader much of novels or poetry, which will always be a form of confession or philosophy, I don't wonder. He's not a believer then?'

Cockerell joins the doctor at the shelves. 'He's always been drawn to places of worship, Doctor, for the history more, I think, and as a young man worked in stones and in draftsmanship on such sites. Likes a good cathedral.'

'His father was a stonemason,' says Barrie.

'Stones are his friends, and animals,' says Cockerell. 'Almost excessive on those. Once as a boy crawled into a sheep pen on all fours, just to see what it felt like, to be a sheep.'

Barrie raises his glass to the light. 'And was delighted to learn that as a baby, a snake was found curled up with him in his cradle!'

'Extraordinary,' says the doctor.

'I think his creed,' says Cockerell, 'is the basic indifference of the universe, Doctor. No malignity, just unknowable, without purpose, without pattern except that of the natural cycle of things. It's a view I find personally sympathetic. And one which finds no fault in fine whisky!'

The doctor had crossed the room again to the fire. 'And morality?'

Cockerell says, 'Not ascribed to any Prime Mover, is that what you ask? Accused of bleakness, indeed accused—who was it said that?—of calling God a vast imbecility, he made the correction that the Cause of Things is neither moral nor immoral but unmoral.'

'But which doesn't let each of us off the hook, Sydney,' says Barrie. 'Ethical action for Tom is always freshened in small individual acts, inscribed there, I believe. Within each of us.'

The doctor nods at this. 'A personal godliness.'

Barrie puts down his glass. 'There's a moment when Jude—his last novel, Doctor—when Jude as a boy steps over the earthworms so as not to disturb their lives. To think of that beautiful scene makes me want to look on his face once more—which I will not attempt, I promise, though I hope to see him in the morning.'

'The arts are not my field. Earthworms, you say? Important to the soil. Well, I must go.' Dr Mann nods and turns to leave.

'Good night, sir,' says Barrie.

'I may see you again before daylight.'

Cockerell accompanies him to the door. 'Your service, Doctor, has made a great difference. Florence has spoken often about it to me. Thank you for everything.'

After the doctor has gone, Barrie looks into the fire. 'I don't think he appreciated the earthworms,' he says.

Cockerell is reading the sheets of paper. 'On the whole I think I prefer my doctors to be utterly unpoetic.' He holds the pages up. 'This one's about George Moore, and this one Chesterton.'

'Why is he thinking of those men now?'

'To put them in their place. Listen. "The literary contortionist/Who prove and never turn a hair/That Darwin's theories were a snare.../And if one with him could see/He'd shout his choice word 'Blasphemy'". A cry for rationalism, right at the end. Moore attacked him some time ago, and he was very annoyed with G. K. over some slight. Tom never forgets.'

'We should celebrate, I know, the forcefulness of such a mind but his sensitivity frankly can seem...well, fine-tuned.'

Cockerell laughs. 'What was it Gosse said? "It's vexing that Hardy feels a pea under the seven mattresses of our admiration."'

'His place is assured. He must know it. His reputation.'

'He feels old-fashioned.'

'He's venerated and loved, Sydney.'

'As an old uncle is. As an old Victorian. His grandmother was around at the time of the French Revolution. Who was it said they were off to visit the ruin at Max Gate? They do have a go at him, the young 'uns.'

'Not just the young 'uns. I met with Gosse a few months ago after he'd been down here. I asked him how it had gone and he said that he and Tom had colloqued merrily of past generations, like two antediluvian animals sporting in the primeval slime.'

'My, he does lay it on a bit thick, doesn't he.'

'Primeval slime, Sydney, is that where we are?'

Cockerell is tucking the two sheets of paper into his jacket pocket.

Barrie sees this. 'What are you doing with those?'

'Here begins the Hardy archive. I tell you, Barrie, from

what I've seen, Tom's entire study is made of paper. All those letters, drafts of poems, and who knows, another novel? It's all there, I'm sure. And having had Florence as secretary all these years, it shouldn't be in any sort of mess.' He points his finger up to the ceiling. 'There's gold in those hills!'

'What are you, a prospector?'

'I'm a co-executor is what I am, with an obligation to posterity.'

'Prosperity too, no doubt.'

'Oh, there'll be sums attached.'

'Well you better hope the other executor thinks as you do.'

'Why, has she said something?'

'Nothing, but Florence's orderliness and care might extend to a certain tidying up of Tom's name, a guarding of his reputation. Tom's had burn-offs before, you know. The chaperoning of an image requires ruthlessness.'

Cockerell comes close to Barrie. 'She's shown you things that might require ruthlessness?'

'No, in fact what she's shown me are the piles and piles of invitations and requests for Tom. The begging letters. And people do come, Sydney. Americans! You yourself have been one of his chief protectors, the man on the gate, otherwise the house would be overrun. Every day new evidence of esteem and affection. He told me when he walks out the door to get his letters, there's frequently someone looking, hoping for a glimpse. They perch in trees. A fellow climbed the wall one time.'

'He's a curiosity, he's become ceremonial, a stop on the tour.'

'He's given this part of the country its renown.'

'Yes, yes, don't worry, I had the local reporter on the doorstep today claiming Tom for the district.'

'He's never left them and they return that loyalty.'

'Oh come now, my dear Barrie.'

'Why?'

'When Emma Hardy was alive, he criticised her for what he called "running around after local people". In truth, I don't think there's much affection for Tom in these parts no matter what his books have done. There's always been grumbling that he hasn't done enough locally. He hasn't exactly spread the gold.'

'Grumblers are everywhere though. And still, here he is. Right to the end. He never left them, did he.'

'He's left them all right. Whenever he wanted a life, Barrie, then he left them! The places in London, the escapes. This Lord of the Manor stuff is in danger of being overplayed. The observer of the seasons, well, quite. But the London season meant as much to him, as we know. Society meant as much. Balls and parties! Opening nights!'

'It's true he came to many of mine.'

'Actresses! Dowagers! Travel, the continent. The wider world. We forget the wider world at a cost. I mean you and me. And at this crucial time, we should consider all options.'

'What do you mean, Sydney?'

'I mean the burial.'

'At Stinsford, with Emma and his parents. I've seen the spot.'

Cockerell goes to the table and pours himself another whisky. 'I mean that, yes.'

'Which will need to be managed given the huge interest. People will certainly be climbing the trees for a vantage.'

'Given the interest, yes. Will you have another?' He holds up the bottle to Barrie, who shakes his head.

'Since Stinsford is in his will and completes the circle,' says Barrie.

'As he's often said, yes.'

Barrie takes out a cigarette and lights it from an ember at the front of the fire. 'What options, Sydney?'

Cockerell comes forward and Barrie gives him a cigarette, lighting it from his own. 'We shan't pretend the subject hasn't arisen before.'

'The Abbey.' Barrie blows smoke at the fire, making it glow in parts and a puff comes into the room. He waves it away with his hand.

'I have been in contact with the Dean.'

'Westminster Abbey.'

'Preliminary inquiries is all.'

'With Tom's knowledge?'

The Cock has found something in his drink, a tiny bit of ash, and fishes for it with his finger. 'On his behalf. I've carried for some time, it's not a boast, well, hardly his imprimatur. But I've seen to things beyond them both, beyond Tom and dear Florence.'

'There's been no one put there in Poets' Corner since—'

'Since Tennyson, yes. Dickens was the last novelist. Tom is the most important English writer of the last fifty years, more. It seems likely the Prime Minister would be interested.'

'You're through to Baldwin?'

'Indirectly. It's a national event. The Prince of Wales

has come for tea and sat in this very room. William Butler Yeats drank from these glasses too.'

The Sprite inspects his glass. 'But Sydney, Tom's will. Florence. His brother. Kate. Everyone!'

'They've said they wouldn't put him under the floor, where Dickens and Tennyson are, but in an urn.'

'Cremation!' In the light of the fire, Barrie's face is pink, glittery, stretched, like the gland of some suckling animal.

'The urn would be carried within a special casket, so we could do pallbearers. They don't want to dig up the floor. He would be in Westminster Abbey, James. With the immortals. I feel we stand at an important moment in time, to decide this for our friend. It's weighed heavily on me for weeks, months. To share it with you gives me some comfort.'

Barrie throws his cigarette into the fire and swallows his drink. 'It gives me little, Sydney.'

'Testament to the delicacy of the situation, I agree.'

'Testament to the impossibility of the situation. Do we have a right?'

'The genius of Thomas Hardy, I believe, lies in the universal.'

'And his body in the embrace of his family and of his birthplace.'

'He will always be the son of this place! But the books that are his life's work allow him to father any number of children and for generations to come—we readers are those children. And the great Abbey, in the great city, is the place to acknowledge his paternity.'

Barrie laughs sourly. 'You make it sound like a custody case.'

'It is one. Isn't it our duty to give him to all of the people—for that is the kind of generosity I believe to have animated his literature and his life. The boy, the boy Jude, who steps over the…the…what were they?'

'Earthworms.'

'The worms, yes, so as not to disturb their lives, is as you say a beautiful creation, but it is that boy's creator whose image we should now promote into its rightful prominence. The Abbey is a stage and Hardy has earned the call-up. I need your support in this, James.'

'Why?'

'As a friend. As J. M. Barrie. Creator of Peter Pan. Sir James. The beloved Barrie.'

'And?'

'Well.'

'Because of Florence. You think I could persuade Florence?'

'I think you have a position, my dear Barrie.'

'If I have it is not of my seeking and none of my doing.'

'Nevertheless. One remembers the story you told me of her attendance at your play.'

'Dear Brutus, the matinée. Years ago.' He goes to the table and pours himself another whisky.

'That having broken down, she sought comfort,' says Cockerell. 'And since that time, a special relationship has come about, of the strictest propriety, but deep.'

The Barrie drinks. 'Deeper in her mind.'

'She listens to you.'

'She was very low. Tom was publishing those poems about Emma again. My play was about the "might-have-beens" of life. It touched a chord.'

'She has great affection for you. They both have.'

'This is impossible, Sydney.'

Cockerell picks up the poker and stirs the fire. 'I'm asking nothing. Nothing except that this life gets a good curtain. We all need a good curtain. A good curtain can save a bad play, you've said it yourself.' There is a loud pop and something jumps onto the carpet. Cockerell looks for it but can't see it. Hurry now! The carpet is singeing. Barrie comes forward quickly and steps on it. He winces as if feeling it through his shoe.

'Thank you,' says Mr Cockerell.

The curtain closes on its smooth rail. I feel it in my head, presumably behind my eyes. A moment of darkness and hush.

Alice carries a pot and a scrubber out the backdoor. His bicycle appears at the back gate. Poor Alex, he had great skill with shooting, all sorts of things. But finally he was shot. What he brought to Max Gate by way of animals he'd trapped or shot had to be done under cover since Mr Hardy had expressly banned Bert Stephens or any of us from dealing to any life-form that came within the house's orbit, no matter how destructive it was to fruit or vegetables. It drove Bert mad to watch the hares dining on his hard work.

Alex calls to Alice gently.

'Oh! Mr Peters! Another ghost to shorten my life.'

'What's happened, Alice?'

She approaches the gate and speaks to him through the

railings. 'He didn't eat his bacon. Just picked at it. But said my broth was the thing, and ate some of it.'

'I hope it was killed right.'

'What was?'

'The pig from whence the bacon came, Alice. Your Mr Hardy likes a humane killing. He's signed up for the Wessex Saddleback Pig Society. They're using his name.'

'I don't know what you're on about.'

'Never mind. Then what happened?'

'Then the doctor came and ate a lot of it. What are you here for, Mr Peters? It's late. I don't like it and am going inside. Nellie won't speak to you, I'm sure.'

'How are you sure of that? Because you've been speaking about me, I suppose.'

'Suppose away.'

'Anyway, did she read to him, Mrs Hardy?'

'He takes a poem or two, not saying much. I can't be talking to you, you know. Mr Cockerell said a thing to Cook that maybe he knew and said it was serious if any person was taking the events beyond these doors.'

'Cockerell will take him to Westminster Abbey. He'll take Mr Hardy.'

'For a last look? The journey would kill him!'

'To be buried there, Alice.'

'At the Abbey?'

'They'll take him to London once he's gone.'

'It's where everyone ends up I suppose.'

'In his will, Mr Hardy is at Stinsford. With his family.'

'Ah.'

'But Cockerell wants him grander than that.'

'Of course, he's the Cock.'

'The cock-a-hoop,' says Alex.

Alice looks into her pot, which is dull with a thin glinting slice of light at its bottom, like the narrow body of a fish. 'Stinsford's nice. I've never been to London and don't want to, having come this far and not suffered greatly for it. Nellie will be gone in a flash. Up to London and that's the last we'll see of her, both of us.'

'What do you mean?'

'I mean Mrs Florence won't be hanging around here afterwards.'

He thinks for a moment. 'Alice, when something happens, when it happens—'

'I'll shut my ears and eyes.'

'No. You'll tell me.'

'I'll tell ye nothing, Mr Peters. Since Mr Cockerell spoke to Cook.'

'Mr Cockerell is the one who'll take Mr Hardy.'

'Don't believe you! He can't. Not everyone can go to London, it's not right, Mr Peters!'

'Watch 'em.'

'I won't. I'll be gone too.'

'Where?'

'Somewhere. I don't know. Maybe I'll be tossed on the street.'

'After all you've done.'

'I've worked hard.'

'I've seen that.'

'It's not been easy, you know.'

'The house is a hard one, I imagine.'

'The hardest.'

'And you've stayed loyal.'

'I have.'

'There's the Bockhampton connection too, with your mother.'

'How'd ye know about that?'

'I take an interest.'

'My mother was born at Bockhampton same as he was.'

'Precisely.'

'They want us to shave him!'

'They'll get you to agree to anything.'

'But he does need it, Mr Peters. You see his poor chin above the blankets, like a badger. Who could bear to touch the ends of that moustache.'

'It's a hard hard time you're all having.'

'It's such a caddle. I don't know what to think or do.'

'Follow your conscience.'

'Oh that's simple then, my conscience.'

'Think of what's best.'

'Font of wisdom, aren't ye.'

'You're right, Alice, I know very little. But I do know you're a good person and will do the right thing, bearing in mind all the connections your family has, and all the loyalty you've shown.'

'It was me who was suspicious of the Chinaman.'

'What Chinaman?'

'A few months ago a Chinaman turned up at the door. Very well-dressed, a gentleman. But I was doubtful. He'd come to see Mr Hardy. And later I heard Mrs Florence and she was very unhappy Mr Hardy had agreed to meet him. I made him wait on the doorstep.'

'It's that sort of vigilance which is so valuable.'

'He didn't look right. He looked like a spuddler.'

'A spuddlin' bugger!'

'Hark at ye!'

'What did he want?'

'No idea, just to meet Mr Hardy, I think, as everyone does. So we're all told to be on guard, to protect him. Otherwise the place would be run off its feet with every sod who wants in.'

'You do a great job.'

'Plus—'

'What?'

'Oh, I was just thinking, I used to have lovely hands.'

'Show me them.'

'Don't be daft! I won't show them now. Not that horror show. I'm away inside now.'

Alice hurries inside. His bicycle wheels off Mr Peters, the single beam of light ending in the trees along the path. The things hoot wisely. Hurry! They must have sensed it. How could God not have believed in either them or him?

F., in her nightgown, stands outside the door of T. H.'s bedroom, listening. A muffled, laboured room, breathing. Hear it? At her feet, Wessex sleeps pressed hard against his master's door. Along the hallway, it opens and James steps out. They see each other. For a moment, neither one knows what to do. Then she moves towards him.

'I couldn't sleep,' she says.

'No. Is there someone…?'

'Eva.'

'Dear Eva.'

'We were taking turns, only now Dr Mann has forbidden me to, says I must rest.'

'Good advice,' he says. 'But hard.'

'The hardest thing I've ever done. I am never so happy as when I have someone to take care of. Does that sound terribly selfish?'

'Not at all, my dear.'

'I married him to express my devotion and because the thought of leaving Max Gate was unbearable, leaving him alone and quite helpless, as he was back then after Emma died. You do understand the nature of my connection with Tom?'

'No one questions your devotion.'

'I would rather be that poor animal sleeping right there outside his door.' They both look at Wessex, the rise and fall of his little tufty belly, his tail twitching. 'It's so wonderful of you to be here, James.'

'Nonsense. An honour.'

'It lifts him too, to know that you're close. It lifts us all.' She drops her head. 'Where were you going?'

'Oh, I'm not quite sure now. A walk perhaps, something.'

'Yes, something.'

'It's snowing again, I believe.'

'But where would you walk to in this weather, at this time?'

'Just around the house, a wee circuit.' He smiles. 'I like the snow.'

'Do you? Will you be warm enough? I'd hate you to get ill. You have your weak chest too.'

'Kind of you to think of that now but I'm feeling well enough.'

'Do you know the last trip Tom made was in October. I told him it was too cold to be out but he insisted. Off we went to Fordington, where they'd found a Roman pavement. He was desperate to see what they'd uncovered, and a bitter north wind was blowing, but he stood there and listened to the explanations and he stooped down in the mud where they were digging. I mark that as the beginning of this decline. Why didn't I put my foot down and tell him he couldn't go?'

'Because he's Tom.'

'Because he's stubborn as you are stubborn. Do you have a scarf at least?'

'It's a very gentle night with the wind dropped.' He steps closer to her. 'But you must really stop worrying about others all the time and look after yourself. You must try to sleep, dear Florence.'

She nods and smiles. 'Good night.' Then she moves alongside him and touches his arm. 'I dread missing it and I dread seeing it.'

A waking sound from Wessex makes them step apart. One eye opens and closes.

Finally I'm in bed under the blankets though still dressed, for warmth and because it doesn't seem our duty is ended yet. Alice is lying beside me. She's told me about holding the knife as Mrs F. came close in the kitchen, and about Alex's visit and his pestering, as she calls it. This tiredness I feel, strangely, makes me happy, or just careless perhaps, slightly delirious anyway and it's enjoyable listening to

Alice complain. Lying on the bed with another warm body beside mine, I find that mention of Alex's name doesn't aggravate me or make me tense. Alice's body, where we touch at the shoulders and legs, acts as an appliance—a domestic appliance!—for drawing off my anxiety. It's a simple pleasure to be physically connected like this. At the same time I feel Alice's nearness is like Alex's. She doesn't banish him by being with me. She's not instead of him. With her here, I'm deeply reminded of him. This should be confusing but it isn't. The memory of his body is wholly straightforward, fun, and connected obviously to the period before things crashed. I feel light, free, and nor do I wish him here. Alice is perfect. If he were to walk in, none of this lightness would remain. Thinking this, thinking how he affects me, makes me resent him.

It's so cold.

'Do you think it will happen tonight?' says Alice. She asks every night. Answering herself, using my regular reply, she says, 'Maybe, maybe not.'

'I think it's very close,' I say. 'Very close.' I don't want to tell Alice about mending the coat in F.'s room since it will only make her jealous.

'But what will happen to him afterwards?' She props herself on one elbow and looks at me.

'One thing's for certain, he won't care.'

'But Nellie, is that the important thing?'

'It's the true thing.'

'Is what he wanted before he goes, is that important too?'

I laugh.

Alice is affronted, which takes me by surprise. It makes

me think of Ma. Suddenly I don't feel good at reading people, a skill I thought I had. Or the people are so scrambled, they won't be read. They're all in Latin. It's the end of the English world.

'You don't think I care?' she says.

'Dearie, I know you care. Just not our business, is it.'

Alice drops onto her back again. Her fury is new. What have I missed?

She says, 'You could speak to her.'

'To Mrs Hardy? And say what?'

'That you're worried, that you hope things will be worked out so that Mr Hardy gets to rest at Stinsford, where he wants and where he belongs.'

'And she'll listen to me, will she?'

'I'm not saying she will or she won't, only that you'll have done the right thing. But if that's not important anymore then—'

'The right thing at this moment is to wish for Mr Hardy's longevity on account of the fact he's still with us.'

'You sound like someone else, not yourself, Nellie. Why would you carry on saying that nonsense. I hope it's not for my benefit, that you think I can't accept he's a goner. I gave him his tea today. I know.'

'And he ate something, did he not?'

'The tiniest amount.'

'He ate something.'

'Really, I now wonder if it's you who's in denial. Everyone else sees what's coming, Nell. I'm surprised, I am.'

'Don't be. I just don't like people getting ahead of themselves. If Alex has been putting ideas into your head—'

'Ideas? So ye are worried now I might be better informed. You preferred me when I was stupid, did ye.' She swings her legs off the bed and stands up.

I sit up in bed. 'What Alex Peters wants is to have a scoop. He wants to be the first newspaperman to know that Thomas Hardy is dead. That's all. He's thinking of himself and his career, don't you worry about Alex Peters.'

'Just angry with him is what you are.'

'I am angry with him, that's true. He's a lying cheating bastard, as we both know. But I'm also angry with him because he's taking advantage of ye.'

'Worried he might fall for me, is that it?' She looks spiteful now, red in the face.

'Don't be daft.' I laugh again.

'So I'm daft to think he might be attracted to me?'

'I've seen what he goes for. He could be attracted to a lamp-post if he thought it would get him places.'

She has tears in her eyes. Of course she's stuck on him. 'You're a mean witch, Nellie! Things go wrong for ye and ye try to spoil it for everyone!'

'If you want to be with Alex Peters, Alice, be my guest. I've moved out of that residence for good.' I feel stupid sitting in bed saying such things and so I stand up, knocking over the candle on the floor. I snatch it up. It's still alight.

'Then why even say horrible things about him? You're a poisoner and don't care for anyone except yourself. Certainly ye don't care if they take Mr Hardy to London. That's your plan!' She points wildly at me. 'Oh my God, I just worked it out. If he goes to London, that's all the more reason for her to leave the house. There'd be no reason to stay in the district, would there, and she'd take you with her. That's how you're playing it. Very cosy. You'll all be in London, living the life!'

'Yes, that's right, I've had it planned all along. I've been working with Mr Cockerell and Sir James Barrie for some time now. They're very keen on getting me to London with Mrs Hardy and so they're arranging it right now with Westminster Abbey. It's been years in the planning but we're almost there. How clever of you to have worked it out, Alice. We underestimated you, I see that now. I must ring the Archbishop and tell him we need another plan, this one's been rumbled.'

'That's not what I mean,' she cries.

'Then what do you mean?' Wax drips on my fingers with a pain that flares and leaves.

'You're twisting it!'

'Then twist it back.' Stupidly I'm shaking the stupid candle.

'Oh, you're horrid. You're horrid and nasty.' She slides down the wall and weeps, her arms covering her face.

I'm trembling, vindictive—and also justified. And also ashamed. We stay like this for a few moments—her sobbing, my shaking. I set the candle on the table.

'Alice,' I say. 'Please. I'm sorry. We're both just so tired, aren't we. Don't know what we're saying. Come on now. What are ye crying for?'

She speaks from between her folded arms: 'I don't need a reason.'

'Yes but it's upsetting to see you like this.'

'I'm sorry for upsetting you.'

'Don't be like that.'

'Like what? A stupid idiot? Obviously I can't help it.'

'Don't.'

I move to her and sit beside her on the floor. Finally she bumps her head against my arm. She does it again harder.

'Okay,' I say.

'God I'll be pleased to leave this house,' she says.

'You know there are poems about this house.'

'Don't care.'

'He wrote one about Emma, his first wife. About her living here.'

'Not her, please, Nell.'

'Called it "Lonely Days".'

'There's a surprise.'

Lonely her fate was,
Environed from sight
In the house where the gate was
Past finding at night.'

'Was she drunk then that night?'

'Where the gate was, that's us. Max Gate.'

'Think I got that.'

'Clever girl you.

Never declaring it,
No one to tell,
Still she kept bearing it—
Bore it well.'

'A likely story,' says Alice. 'Bore it well? We all bear it, don't we. Cos what else can we do?'

'Thing was, she went mad, old Emma did.'

'I can believe it too.'

'And this used to be her attic-study.'

'This?'

'She removed herself here and stayed for years. She wrote her memoirs apparently right here. And fumed and fumed.'

'You can smell the fumes.'

'That's the smell!'

'I wish I didn't know she stayed in your room, Nell.'

'Cook told me.'

'Fuck Cook.'

Far off Wessex barks twice, then we hear his sulky whine.

'Shut up,' Alice whispers. 'Shut up, dog.'

Quiet. Wet slaps of snow on the window.

Alice looks at me. 'What? What did I do?'

I shake my head, smiling at her.

'Then why are ye blubbering? What's with the waterworks?'

'Don't know,' I say.

'See,' she says, 'it's this place, Nellie. Mr Hardy has the right idea if you was asking me, getting out when he has the chance.'

We'd done Tintagel and were walking along the cliffs near Beeny. Earlier Alex had told me there was a story that Hardy and Emma were accidentally locked in the castle when they visited it as a courting couple decades before. It had been warm inland, but above the sea it was cool and windy and we walked close together, not yet touching. The story was so obviously romantic, I was surprised—surprised Alex had told it to me when we were at the castle. For some reason I hadn't realised up until that moment that we would sleep together, and perhaps it would happen on that day. I'd been so full of excitement at being away from Max Gate and with Alex, who'd suggested the trip, that I hadn't thought further than the basics: the car (borrowed from Alex's uncle), driving to the coast, eating the picnic food (prepared by me away from the prying eyes of Cook and Alice). The accommodation: Alex had booked two rooms somewhere between so we'd stop off on the way home. That seems unbelievable, that I hadn't done any mental forecasting, but it was true. The story of Emma and Thomas locked up changed all that. I was walking along the cliff over-aware of everything—the feel of the air against the backs of my hands, the saltiness lifting in currents around us, the shadows on the ground ahead from broken clumps of cloud, streaks of white marble in the slate of the cliffs, the rough murky grass and the patches of heather and gorse—and hardly able to take in what Alex was saying. Let him speak, I thought. Look how content he is, how animated and keen on his own knowledge. He was telling me about a peregrine. The last time he'd been here a falcon had settled on a current which was level with his position on the cliff and they'd stayed together like that for ages. And when he walked, the bird flew, holding him in position. I must have been speeding up because at one point he said, is it a race to get there, and I slowed down and laughed. What a strange laugh.

He was puffing. The picnic basket knocked against his knee as he carried it. He had thin legs, then wide feet. In some ways I couldn't take him seriously, he was such a know-it-all. Yet he knew this too—that facts and opinions sprang from him too hectically—so there was irony in his intelligence. Regularly he'd interrupt himself to say, I have no idea why you'd need to hear this. But there was no stopping him. A lot of it was about the Hardys, about whom he knew a great deal. And did I remember the scene in this book or this one? I had to admit I'd never read the books. Never mind, he told me brightly, you were probably doing something much more interesting than reading. I doubt it, I said.

What else about Alex? Think.

He had extremely poor teeth, yes—they crossed in the front in complicated, painful-looking ways—which he didn't try to conceal and somehow this made his face more attractive. I remember thinking he was brave because of this. That he didn't fear ridicule as I constantly did. Not sure why I forgot all this earlier when trying to reconstruct his face in my hands as I remembered holding it. I decided I would have to try not to watch him eat the sandwiches I'd made. What would kissing that mouth be like? His hair was dark and curly, a bit unkempt, the curls falling over his forehead made sense of the teeth. Squiggly patterns.

Did I know the legend of Beeny and Beeny in Disguise?

No, I said, no, stalking ahead so his answer was half blown away.

There was a path down the side of the purplish cliff leading to the beach but Alex had some complicated reasons involving tides which again I failed to follow and we headed away from the Atlantic Ocean, towards a group of trees by a rocky outcrop.

We had the world to ourselves. This felt like the edge of the earth.

Our picnic spot was amazingly sheltered. Alex ate in the same way he talked: openly. I was laughing a lot. He wiped food from his chin. The teeth were definitely a problem. It was like being at a show and being part of the show at the same time. Still, he was careful to ask me about my mother and about my life before Max Gate. He let me speak and always had comments to make. Did I know this family or that? Did I realise that shop was the former site of this important civic structure? In other situations (not many) I'd always felt something methodical about a man's interest. Question one and then question two. Not with Alex. His looseness released us from the routine. I had a sudden admittedly disappointing thought that this meant he wasn't in fact keen on me. Did he see me instead as a pupil? He was a few years older than me. His manner might grow teacherly. Mr Hardy had this aspect too, I thought. Pairing them was not a happy thought.

The sun was hotter and I was feeling drowsy. Alex grew quiet and sat with his back against the tree and closed his eyes. We separated here. I feared again he was drifting away from certain ideas that had brought us to this spot. In closing his eyes he was cutting himself off from me. I wondered if my body wasn't quite as he'd imagined it to be. Was the hair on my arms too dark, nonsense like that? My waist too thick? I closed my eyes and lay back on the picnic blanket in an odd mix of panic and weariness.

My inexperience felt like a curse. Soon I'd be back at Max Gate, helping with the dinner, getting told off.

Then Alex started reciting:

'I see now what you are doing: you are leading me on
To the spots we knew when we haunted here together,
The waterfall, above which the mist-bow shone
At the then fair weather,
And the cave just under, with a voice still so hollow
That it seems to call out to me from forty years ago,
When you were all aglow,
And not the thin ghost that I now frailly follow!'

I told him that was nice and he said he didn't know about nice since it was Hardy's pain at looking for Emma, after she'd died, in the places they'd visited. He said this with just a touch of frustration—his pupil was very slow. The only thing I could remember at that moment was the first line he'd spoken about being led on—this had given me a fright. He's saying I led him on. The feeling I had about the Tintagel Castle story was hard to recapture now. Instead of a romantic delirium, there was the cold assessment of our respective intentions. *Had* I led him on? He'd suggested the trip, decided the itinerary, borrowed the car. Cook had vouchsafed his reputation with Mrs Florence. But hadn't I made the lunch? And hadn't I said yes? This yes was, in the man's view, as wide as the blanket I was lying on. I sat up. At the abruptness of my movement he opened his eyes and stared at me. I didn't look away.

'What's wrong?' he said.

'Nothing.'

'You look very pretty, Nellie, sitting there.'

I almost laughed at this. Surely I'd been scowling. What could I reply? 'It's a beautiful spot.'

'Yes but I think you've improved it.' He moved closer to me.

The terrible formula gripped us. He didn't sound like himself anymore and nor did I. But then why should we? This was new and so were we—new, I mean, to ourselves as well as to each other. I glanced down at the blanket and noticed a faint shiver in his hand resting near mine. It wasn't that this was a routine he was practising; he was afraid. Afraid of me? I took his hand in mine and leaned towards him. We kissed very gently. His face was hot, which meant mine wasn't so much. This gave me confidence. His gentleness was a kind of apology, I believed, for his teeth, the only one he was prepared to make, and only when another person was in close contact with them. Only then was he admitting a physical truth about himself. My response was to press harder, in gratitude. I didn't mind. He was clever. He had poems in his head. He also liked me because I was at Max Gate, I have no doubt about that. Not that he was scheming—the day out to Tintagel was the summer of 1927, a long time before Mr Hardy took seriously ill, and he already knew Cook. Yet my connection to the house was attractive. Certainly he'd asked what I did before Max Gate. I'd been at a house in Kent where my employer, a retired WAAF officer, suffering from the War, often believed I was an orderly and gave me commands in a military manner. Alex laughed but he was only half-listening—this wasn't the story he really wanted.

I'd had two boyfriends before Alex—both short-term and both unsatisfactory. It was always difficult to find venues. Standing up in a lane at midnight behind the old iron yard. Behind a bush by the river. The crinkled waters of the Frome. If I say that with Alex it wasn't memorable, it will sound strange, since I've amassed a surprising amount already. Naturally I remember it happened. But what happened? And how were my feelings involved? Memorability as a test for sex is something I've always been puzzled about. Never having asked Robert—my only lifetime partner (I was about to put 'yardstick'!)—what he remembered of our physical intimacy, I find I'm still lost. Do others think the same as me? The problem here is that my sample is myself. Where are the women to whom I might have spoken about this?

You are asleep, remembering sex. You almost laugh in your bed.

For the next week I remember feeling on edge. Alex came once to Max Gate in that week, to deliver something for Cook probably. I only heard he'd been after he'd left. Hearing that, I experienced a surge—God, this language is awful. Thinking: look at you, you would have torn his arms off. I felt if he came within reach, we would tear at each other. This proved to be the case. I had the key to Bert Stephens' shed. The risk seemed both very large and very small, since it was on the property but unvisited except when Bert was working his three days a week. I chose the afternoon when both Alice and Cook were away. Look, Alex said, pointing where the faint outline of names ran down the shed door. I'd noticed them before and thought they were the marks of children—but what children? Max Gate wasn't a place for or of children. These are German names, Alex said, from the War, when prisoners came to work in the garden. He seemed to know everything.

I asked if he knew about the Roman relics in the house. He did but not the details. He knew things had been sent to the British Museum. We went inside the shed and he said, so are you going to tell me? Tell you what, I said. About the Roman relics. What though? Details, he said, details! Oh, can I remember? Try, he said. If you don't mind. They've never let me in the front room, he said. No, you have to be very special to get in there, I told him. Will you tease until I'm crazy, Nell? You're crazy already to be so fixated on all things Hardy. I admit I am, he said. Relieve me anyway. Thought that's why we were here in the first place, I said. Pressure builds in various places, he said, smiling, sometimes even in the mind. Well, I said, there's a Roman lady's fibula, and once I heard Mr Hardy tell a guest about a small clip. He said, 'I took this from a female skull, where it had evidently fastened a band around the head.' Alex said, you do his voice pretty well. All that practice in listening to it, I said. 'Thomas A Didymus had a black beard; Kissed all the maidens and made 'em a feard.' What's that from? Alex asked. Some old thing, I think. 'Thomas A Didymus King of the Jews/Jumped into the fire and burnt both his shoes.' Was he King of the Jews, said Alex. No idea, I said.

Later, lying in the tiny bed that Bert took his afternoon naps on, I recited:

'A little old man and I fell out
How shall we bring this matter about?
Bring it about as well as you can,
Get you gone, you little old man!'

What are you? said Alex. Some poet yourself?

It was that power I felt—to make things, to announce things. Even if it was only old nursery rhymes. I said: ye think the only one who can recite is ye?

'Old woman, old woman, shall we go a shearing?
Speak a little louder, sir, I am very thick of hearing.
Old woman, old woman, shall I kiss you dearly?
Thank you, kind sir, I hear you very clearly!'

One other thing from that picnic day, which at the time I thought—not sure what I thought. Clearly it was not enough to ruin anything. Here it is: as we were lying together under the trees a bird hopped nearby. Very playfully. Probably trying to get at the crumbs from our lunch. Hello, I said. Hello, little bird. Then Alex put an imaginary rifle to his eye and, making a trigger with his fingers, he shot it. Off it flew at the sound his lips made. I don't think he was doing it to impress me or warn me or put me off him. We'd enjoyed too much for that, seen each other's pleasure. So why shoot? I think it was a reflex. I think as a boy this is what he did and he was still doing it. A bird lands nearby and is shot. I thought then: you are not the one. No matter all of this—the peregrine, the cloud shadows on the heather, the shivering hand—you are not the one.

Do you know the significance of Mr Hardy putting his arm into water and why it is you must carry the water up to him for his hip bath so he can repeat the ritual? It's because when he and Emma Hardy were courting, they picnicked in the Valency valley and she had to reach into the water of a miniature waterfall to try to retrieve a tumbler that had fallen in. She couldn't get it, and so he tried, but to no avail. The tumbler was lost somewhere between the rocks. And when she died, he became obsessed with this moment and this place and this action—reaching one's arm into water, trying to find something that's gone, that though it feels so near and within range, is ungraspable. And that is why, with the risk of injury, you must carry the water up those stairs to him.

Let me feel your pulse, sir. Cold hands, sorry.

Florence was sitting at her table at that moment, opening the letters, working by a lamp which doesn't give much light. She has three distinct piles in front of her and she allots each letter to one of the piles. Urgent. Non-urgent. Ignore. This is exactly what she did before she was his wife. And suddenly she has the sensation that someone is sitting nearby, watching her.

Emma would come and sit with her sometimes, ostensibly to look over the correspondence, though her interest in this in the final years was nil. She grew to regard any envelope bearing the name Thomas Hardy as repellent and couldn't bear to be around 'all these pieces of paper'. But earlier on, she didn't mind Florence and the letters. She'd sit and aggressively reminisce about her childhood and youth in Plymouth. The upper windows of their house with glorious views etcetera. Moonlit nights, she and her sister slept with the blinds up and they could see the fishing boats in the harbour. Was she tormenting herself? Florence listened or half-listened, wondering at the depths of this woman's ingratitude. Mrs Hardy seemed dim, quite unaware of what she had, what she was living with, and who. There was a tortoise existing happily in the garden of the Plymouth house when Emma was a girl. Even the phrase 'when I was a girl' seemed to be used as an act of aggression, a synonym for 'when I was happy'. Or perhaps that's why we remember anything, Florence thought after several sessions, with a jolt of unhappiness.

There was never a hint that Florence should share her childhood.

Emma's memories were excruciatingly detailed: the tame seagull who lived in the front garden (tortoise in the back) feasting on kitchen cockroaches or dead kittens (from where?) or meat and bread scavenged from neighbouring houses. 'He was not particular in his appetite, which was of the gorging kind, and most friendly.' Friendly? Eating kittens? 'There was a bee settlement by one of our top windows and a man came and took it away. That was just one of a curious set of omens, fulfilled in due course.'

Florence found that if she listened too carefully to Emma's rantings, she felt dizzy and almost ill. It was far better to have something of her own to think about, to fill her mind with noise of her own. She tried to think of letters to publishers she had to write the following day. She tried to remember addresses and titles of the people she would write to. Anything.

'There was a curious craze for sea-anemones then, everybody talking of, and collecting them.'

The problem was Emma's voice was peculiarly penetrating, even when she was telling Florence that she thought the substitution of five o'clock tea instead of the silver tray brought in for afternoon visitors with rich cake, biscuits, port and sherry as early as three o'clock was a good change. Some change was good. But there was a lot that was to be lamented.

Wessex starts up again. Florence looks in the direction of the barking.

'Wessex!' she calls out. 'Quiet! Wess!'

The dog stops and she resumes her work. Remember the time Wessex was acting strangely around the man—what was his name?—Wilson? Walker? He was the Secretary to the Society of Dorset Men in London and Tom felt obliged. We had afternoon tea. Wessie was whining oddly, circling the fellow. Mr Watkins! And as he went to leave, the dog touched him solicitously on the sleeve with his paw. The gentleman was amused and bent down to pat him but Wessex cringed away, as he never did. Usually he stands erect and butts against the hand or snaps at it. He flings himself one way or another, always casting a clear vote. Not this time. Had he ever been so undecided? A few hours later there was a phone call and again, unusually,

Wessex was quiet. He always barks when the phone rings. The message was from Mr Watkins's distressed sister. The poor man had collapsed suddenly and died in their Dorchester lodgings.

She scans a letter from an American journalist wishing to meet Mr Hardy at his earliest convenience 'to discuss a range of topics suggested by a close reading of the "magnificent cycle of novels" and perhaps to canvas a few more personal questions'. Ignore. Don't like journalists or Americans; American journalist is a category of special toxicity.

As a young woman Emma regularly went to gypsy fortune-tellers who never failed to provide her with prophesy that was 'flattering' (unlike her poor sister) and always true. The family had an old servant (seventy when she died) who also told fortunes and one hot summer's day at twelve o'clock precisely, this servant, called Ann Tresider Chappel, led the two sisters and a parlour-maid to a spot under a tree on the front lawn. Here she brought out three tumblers of cold water and handed out three eggs. 'Each of us then broke our egg, letting the white only drop into the water, then watching what form it would take which should signify the occupation of our future spouses.' In the sister's water appeared a church tower—she would marry a Clergyman. (True.)

In the maid's a ship in full sail—sailor. (True.)

With Emma's, old Ann peered a long time at the shape in the water and then she said, 'See, it's an ink-bottle and a quill pen.' They looked and indeed they could see these things. It was plain. 'You, Emma, will marry a writer.'

Emma said to Florence, 'How my sister hated that and called it all nonsense. Yet it all came true. Now how did those eggs reveal it all?'

More barking.

One evening by the letter-table Emma had told the story of her sister's marriage to the Reverend Cadell Holder, West Indian by birth and delicate as a result. A much older man too. Having completed a rather boring account which involved details of the man's parish, Emma went to leave the room. For some reason Florence asked her a question. Questions were never required. Yet here it was.

'Tell me, Mrs Hardy, how did you come to meet Mr Hardy?' Instantly she flinched with regret.

Emma sat down again. 'Church restoration,' she said, with a smile that Florence found deadly and conceited. Mr Hardy was the assistant architect on the restoration of her brother-in-law's church. Emma was staying with her sister. On the day the architect arrived, the Reverend was laid up in bed with gout and he required the constant attention of his wife. 'So it was just me to welcome this stranger. He'd come from two counties away, changed many trains to be there. In those days, we had a vivid interest in strangers since so few came our way. I remember there was a school inspector one time and—'

Fearing these digressions, Florence heard herself ask: 'And what was he like?'

'Soft voice,' said Emma at once. 'There was a piece of blue paper sticking out his back pocket.'

'What was it?'

'No idea.'

'Would it have been drawings or plans for the church?'

'Probably. He had a beard which was yellowish.'

'Yellowish?'

'A rather shabby great coat.'

'He was just then making his way in the world,' said Florence, explaining it more to herself.

'He seemed familiar.'

'Had you met him before?'

'What? No. As if I'd seen him in a dream.'

Florence recalled the egg whites dropped in the water—a story from another day—and willed herself not to prompt Emma with it.

'We walked around the district a lot. The focus was on the church of course. He came a few times and we corresponded in between times. I rode my pretty mare Fanny all over the coast. The servant-man taught me to jump hurdles on Fanny but Fanny got a little lame and we stopped it. I'd ride and he would walk alongside and I showed him the places I knew, the cliffs, the hamlets, the solemn little shores where the seals lived.'

'The servant-man?'

'Mr Hardy, this is. I'm talking about Tom. Are you paying attention?'

'Sorry.'

'We sketched and talked of books. I remember we went to Tintagel and to Trebarwith Strand. Do you know it? I'm sure it's changed now but there was something upsetting that day, we both commented on it. I believe it was a moment that bonded us more closely.' She paused for so long, with the determined wistfulness Florence found especially galling, that the latter was ready to stand up and leave the room—she'd finished with the correspondence anyway.

Finally, Florence said: 'What was that bond?'

'The local farmers employed donkeys to carry seaweed up from the beach. We watched these poor burdened animals, huge loads of dripping, smelling seaweed on their bare backs, struggling through the shingle and then up the steep path from the sea. It was a hot day and they worked without rest or shade. A group of boys from some family party were laughing at the donkeys and clapping their hands to give them a fright. Down on the beach a few farmhands lashed at the donkeys to keep them moving. It was horrible, cruel. Yet everyone involved found it normal, even amusing. Tom was very angry and he saw how I was affected too, which made him angrier. He told the boys to move away from the animals and he spoke with such power, they did, running off. From then, we knew we shared a view of how things should be in a better world. The farmhands we could do nothing about. It was simply their work. The sea-spray whipped up around them until they almost disappeared. They were like ghosts down the beach, raising their arms and striking out. We left that spot deeply disturbed and hardly spoke on the way home.'

Florence was standing now, tidying the papers one last time. She felt in listening to Emma she'd punished herself. She needed to be punished. It was wrong for her to be in this position. She should leave Max Gate. She would hand in her notice. Another secretary could be found. She would go home to look after her mother. Eva could take a break.

Emma wasn't finished, however. 'That blue piece of paper.'

'What?' said Florence, flustered, looking around on the desk.

'The piece of paper Tom had in his back pocket

when we first met. It wasn't a plan or anything. It was the manuscript of a poem.'

'Oh!'

'Yes! Which greatly surprised me and intrigued me, I must say. Because that was one thing I wondered about. If my spouse, by prophesy, was to be a writer, who was this architect? When I found out he carried a poem in the back pocket, I knew it was okay. It was all coming true.'

After Emma died, Tom asked that they meet to discuss what would happen with Mrs Hardy's things. Florence thought he meant her clothes and personal items and that she was being engaged as a female, but it became clear he had no interest in these. He meant her papers—her writings and drawings. He wished Florence to catalogue them. He'd started to read her diaries, he said, and was profoundly moved by them. When as part of this task she came to read them, she discovered they were diabolical. Pages of diatribe and falsehood aimed at her husband. Mr Hardy liked to carry these diaries around in his pocket and read aloud from them. One passage, she recalled, supposedly recorded the opinion of Emma's father that Tom was worthless, weak and not to be trusted. He would read these vile entries and then immediately begin on an account of his deceased wife's countless virtues and graces. Despite knowing that Florence had witnessed many times Emma's deranged hostility, he would continue with his praise. Florence understood the need to substitute this suffering saint for the real-life version who'd made the past decade such a torment for everyone at Max Gate. But she could not understand—or even tolerate—the abject self-abasement of these diary readings or the pretence that she,

Florence, had not witnessed Emma's awfulness first-hand. As a tactic Florence actively discouraged potential well-wishers from mentioning the dead wife since the merest mention set off these aggravating lamentations.

Suddenly there's a scream—single and quickly hushed—and Florence drops the letter she's holding. There are feet, the sound of running voices, and the dog going again. She can't move.

Someone is knocking at the door. That they should bother to knock, it's the strangest thing of all that's about to happen, is it? That they—whoever is there—having run in blind terror, should pause and knock. And now be waiting on the other side. Waiting for what? Excuse me, ma'am, but I was wondering if you'll be coming to Mr Hardy's room in the next short while since there seems to be a development that concerns you? Is that the message? And knocking a second time. Who could that person be, this monster of composure. How wonderful too, she suddenly thinks, that the knocking on her door remains in place when everything else is shattered. The kindness of it gives her a sudden boost. The power of movement returns to her. Could it be Barrie? Hello James. Ah, James. Is it over? She walks to the door.

But it's only me.

My throat is utterly closed over.

She stares at me a moment, wide-eyed, wild with insight, I'd say. Or something. Some force erupts in her look, as if she's telling me all that will unfold. A feeling of now and now and now.

She grips my bicep.

'Call the doctor,' she says. 'Call Dr Mann, Nellie. And

then see to Wessex, and make sure he doesn't go upstairs.'
The look again. 'Do you understand?'

I must have nodded.

'You must also tell Sir James and Mr Cockerell, if they haven't already been alerted by the racket. We should also think of the press but not immediately.'

'Yes,' I said.

'Who is the chap who comes?'

'Where?'

'Who is the chap from the local paper who comes to the house, who brings Cook the game? With the bad teeth.'

'That's Alex Peters.'

'Okay, I shall tell Mr Cockerell to contact Alex Peters. But not now.'

'No.'

'Is it snowing?'

'I'm not sure, I don't think so.'

'Nellie, you must ride to Kate and Henry's house.'

'When?'

'Now. If we wait till the morning that will always be held against us. I can't give the task to Alice. Can you take the bicycle, if it's not too dark. You'll have the light on it anyway. Ride there. Can you do that?'

'I can go at once.'

'Tell Kate and she will tell Henry. If Henry answers the door, ask to speak to Kate. She'll be expecting someone. Then come back and tell me that it's done.'

'I will.'

'Good.'

She hesitates and there's just the slightest quiver on her bottom lip, the quickest flash of incomprehension and fright across her face. I should have moved then—towards her, I mean. But was it mine, this moment? No, she would have done it herself if it was what she wanted or needed. She didn't. She was in some management realm again, lifted by the crisis into a state of calm we hadn't seen for weeks and feared was permanently gone from her repertoire. It was impressive, reassuring, and I admired her. I was also repelled once more. If she didn't need to be hugged, did it cross her mind to think I might need that? I felt I did, standing there. My eyes were moist, I knew it. Thomas Hardy was dead. A man was lying dead in Max Gate. Hold me.

Then, with an action I always recall whenever I think of the name Florence Dugdale Hardy, she turns back into the room and slowly closes the door behind her.

Cockerell was quickly dressing himself. He's rushing to get ready and finds he's not done those ones, the right buttons. He must start again. Slow down, old chap, slow down. Then he can't find his other shoe. He looks under the bed. He stands up, lost. Catching himself in the mirror, he's curious about one thing: that grin. Someone stupid might think it was pleasure. It's just this feeling for which there's no name, which comes with bad news, which means the story is advancing.

Barrie was brushing at the sleeves of his jacket. He looked perfect. Like a schoolboy, but old. He reaches for the doorhandle, then pauses and turns back for one last check in the mirror. How haggard he feels, and yet it's not showing. Here is the painting of his good looks. He runs his hand through his hair and nods to himself: right.

Cockerell and Barrie come out of their rooms at the same time, Cockerell flustered, still threading an arm. They look at each other and nod—not a greeting, more like an agreement. Something, they each feel, has been decided between them in this instant—but what? And is it the same thing? There is the sound of female barking, sobbing, animal noises. Cockerell motions that Barrie should go ahead of him. Barrie moves as invited, then pauses, then indicates that Cockerell has rights. You. After you. No you. They dance downstairs.

Cockerell stands in front of the clock in the hall, checking his watch. 'What time do you have, Barrie?'

'Almost fifteen minutes before nine. We shall always remember the hour.'

'Good, good. I must phone the BBC. Hopefully we're just in time to catch the nine o'clock news.'

The woods are very still, and then suddenly a flurry of movement beneath leaves and twigs. Hurry, little creatures! Everyone is trying to go home. Whenever we walked through these places at night, disturbing things, that was what we thought. Our torch failed and we sang to let them know. Quick insects and fellows! The skittering and panic, desperate for escape. Sorry, we said to them. Silence again. A gunshot of sound. Then silence.

The snake enters the baby's crib.

His bicycle, the beam of light ending in the trees. His hunting gun is strapped across the back of the machine. Poking from the top of one of his panniers, some still-warm thing.

Talbothays isn't a hard ride on a nice day. On a winter night, it stretches and contracts in odd bursts, measured as the light from the bike's headlamp is measured, in jerks, in openings and closings as the road turns, rises, falls. I must have missed Alex by not much at all. He was coming from the other direction. I don't remember a lot of this. Miss Kate Hardy had been dozing, I'm sure, and took the news of her brother without visible emotion. How did you get here, my dear? she asked. She was always curious about things in a slightly mismanaged way. The questions were often beside the point and pursued to their pointless ends. How do you keep the tyres inflated, she asked me. We discussed this for some moments, then she thanked me for coming but did I happen to know the forecast for the next day? She said, I have Tom's christening gown. Also the family bible. I could hear Henry Hardy coming to the door as I rode off. Henry died later the same year.

*

The gun hasn't woken her. The hallway is dark. There are human noises coming from an animal. Slowly a bedroom door opens a fraction and F. peers out. Sighing creature. In the light from her room, she can see that Wessex is again lying against T. H.'s bedroom door. She creeps along the hallway and from the top of the stairs, she can see in the study downstairs, glimpsing it; he is talking to Sydney. The men's voices are heard but not what they're saying. She watches for a few moments. James looks up and they see each other. She waits, then creeps back to bed, past the sleeping one.

What did God do? Gave her the cancer five years later. Shot Alex Peters after that. Anyone could make a matching list. Is that why I don't want to get up? Because the world's unfair? Boo-hoo. Still. I think: remember the power you had when your job was winding the clocks at Max Gate. With my hand around the mechanism…sometimes it all speeds up and a lot happens, a lot is taken away, and then not much. For long periods we are free. We hardly hear the ticking. These are the times we can collect our things and see where we are. Are we in the woods at night? Are we in our burrows? Who is coming along the road? What is that light? What are they carrying?

Outside, more shooting.

*

By the back stairs there's a painting of his pet rabbit. He did it when he was a boy. Juno. The animal looks at you as you go to and fro from the garden. You are carrying the food right past his nose. It is, we think, a magic painting. Look, the eyes follow ye! He's always hungry. He wants to eat from your hand. He wants to know what happened. Children who visit try to fool the rabbit. They duck down. They creep below. Somehow he always knows, and when finally they look, he's looking back. There's only one way to escape—at night. But then the stairs plunge forward, lit by nothing but that small patch of slightly brighter black.

Quietly moving Alex puts the two bodies on the back step. He listens at the door. Does he peer in the window? Lights are on everywhere. Meaning? The fire in the kitchen looks freshly fuelled. Significance? Cycling off, he looks up at the attic rooms. Dark. Oh Nellie! How foolish we are. The next morning Cook finds them. 'Bless him,' she says. She takes her best knife, holds them by their ears, their legs stuck in the leap position with the mortis. It's so cold in the morning kitchen before our bodies have warmed the air and before the fire properly takes in its blackened cavern and begins to cough sparks.

PART TWO

He puts the milk out, watching it break though the ice, claps his hands at the sheep, 'How are you, friends?' and then he comes to us in his car.

Mr Hardy liked to say to visitors, I bet you're wondering where we hid the body.

Whose body?

The gardener's.

When she was first here, saucers were placed all around the property and eight cats lived in the house and they are buried with all the others in marked graves by the apple trees.

Are you winning the war, Stephens?

It's a good fight, sir.

We're a temporary occupying force.

It's the leaves are my enemy. I use my bayonet on them.

Ha! Good man, good man.

*

At the door Reverend Cowley holds our hands and looks into our faces. 'My dears.' He smells of cat. Taking his coat, fine white and black hairs stick to our clothes. There are scratches on his hands.

When he follows Mrs Florence into the living room, his fingers are locked behind him, reverse prayer, as if asking for something behind his back.

She holds up the newspaper. 'I don't even know what this is for. Why am I carrying it around?'

'Perhaps the obituary, Mrs Hardy,' he says.

'Yes! Of course. Forgive me. Mr Cockerell was pleased. Two columns. The right sort of note.'

'"English literature deprived of its most eminent figure."'

'Was that it?'

'He was done proud, Mrs Hardy.'

They sit down. Alice brings in the tea tray. 'And that will set the tone, Mr Cockerell says, for the others. Are you cold, Reverend? This house is cold. You know Tom refused all the conveniences. Finally he allowed me the telephone, which he hates. Hated.'

'I'm quite fine, Mrs Hardy. And how are you?'

'You know about Westminster Abbey, don't you.'

'I do.'

'Which is a great honour.'

'The greatest.'

'Dear Barrie, Sir James…I think it's been decided well. In the end.'

Reverend Cowley looks at the floor. 'A great honour.'

'Do you agree?'

She watches him lean slowly forward to scratch at his

long shins. He has very dry skin, flaky around his eyebrows.

'Mrs Hardy, I met with Kate and with Henry, who naturally have taken their brother's death as an immense blow.'

'They're very upset with me! They think I should have put a stop to it. Not his dying, I mean, but the other business.'

'There's no blame.'

'Sir James is in London right now. He has the Prime Minister and the editor of the *Times*. You know they didn't let Meredith in, or Swinburne. Everyone is working very hard on Tom's behalf. And they expect me to go against Mr Baldwin and the *Times* and the whole of England!'

'I believe they see the position you are put in, Mrs Hardy.'

'Do they? For myself, strangely, it is not as great a wrench as might have been the case. You see, Reverend, I have been sharing my husband with the world for years. Why not share this?'

He takes a handkerchief from his pocket, presses it carefully to his nose, and then replaces it. A tiny flake of skin turns through the air, falling. 'Kate and Henry took a walk with me at Stinsford.'

'Oh!'

'It had been raining but it stopped and we walked out among the graves. To the family plot.'

He takes off his glasses, polishes them on his sleeve, and goes on sedately, aiming, she feels, in his words, for the pace of the walk they'd made at Stinsford. She sees them on the path. The old couple—brother and sister—supporting each other, the Reverend coming behind them with the gentlest herding motion. Where are the sheep that wander about? 'And Henry remembered something of their father, and of his father. Not large things. Things of little consequence it seemed but somehow necessary for Henry at that moment. Kate knelt before her sister's place. Such tranquil remembrance. A spider's web had formed over the stone. Ah, the wevet, said Kate. The web. And Kate remembered from her brother's talk about one book, his hopes that the human race be shown in it as one great network or tissue which quivers in every part when one point is shaken, like a spider's web if touched. What an image. The connectedness of us all.' He looks out the window, where branches almost touch the glass, moving slightly. 'When sometimes I'm asked about my parish, I begin to talk of Stinsford and the Hardy name comes inevitably, joyfully.'

Mrs Florence covers her face with her hands. 'What should I do, Reverend? Tell me what to do. He lies upstairs, with nothing decided.'

The vicar leans forward in his chair. 'Mrs Hardy, then that offers a chance, if nothing has been decided. No papers signed?'

'None.'

'But all the important people in London?'

'Onside but it's the Dean, Dr Morris, to say yes or no. We wait for Sir James to send word. There's always the chance finally of a refusal on the grounds of spiritual health.'

'Oh?'

'Meredith and Swinburne were both agnostics. The

Abbey refused them. But...this wouldn't present an obstacle to you, Reverend?'

'The plot at my church is long-standing, the arrangement historical and established without...bias. It's where he belongs. Emma Hardy, if you permit the mention...'

At this name, Mrs Florence gains strength in her voice. 'Emma was his wife. And a friend to me when I first came here to help type Tom's work. I had visited Mr Hardy at Max Gate on two occasions, as a devoted admirer, a reader, and Mrs Hardy had not been present and for some reason had not been made aware of my visits or existence. Then when I made her acquaintance in London, she invited me to come down and stay. In so much as I pretended never to have been here before, we deceived her. Which began our friendship, mine and Emma's, within a shadow that I fear has never left these walls.'

'Please, Mrs Hardy, a time such as this will prompt many feelings of unworthiness which are best subjugated within one's private grief. I only meant to suggest that Emma and the others await him in the churchyard. And I always considered Mr Hardy to be basically a Christian and a Churchman.'

'Did you? He liked to play hymns, the more mournful the better. They cheered him up.'

'Your late husband had, I believe, a great instinct for ritual of many kinds.'

'When he was five years old he used to sit on a particular step in the family cottage every evening as the sun set. This step was the spot where the sun flooded the red stair— Venetian red, he told me—and you know what he would do? He would sing a hymn. He would sing Watts's "And now another day is gone".'

'I do hope that all these marvellous stories will be preserved.'

'I don't think there is anyone I have come across, in life or books, with a more pronounced feeling for time. "And now another day is gone", aged five!'

'He found something in the hymns which is quite profound, I think. And that is that—'

She cuts over him: 'We have three grandfather clocks at Max Gate. One in the passageway leading to the kitchen, one in the hall, and this one here.'

He glances at it. 'Very handsome.'

'To complete the house he thought a sundial.'

'There is something about a sundial!' He's spoken brightly.

'They are not at all straightforward, especially if they aren't freestanding. There's the longitude of the site and the alignment of the wall where it's fixed to be calculated. You need absolute precision or else the thing's a disaster.'

The sunniness of the sundial has vanished. 'Oh, I see.'

'He worked it all out of course. But then somehow never—. Anyway, every Monday morning, Tom wound the clocks. Until very recently, when that job passed to—. The maid was doing it. To tell the truth, Reverend, for myself I wouldn't have minded if they all ran down. The noise gets on my nerves.'

'Ah, yes. The ticking.' A light from somewhere catches the silver cake stand and bounces off his glasses. 'A church never has a clock in it.' The thought appears to hit him unhappily.

'Tom thought "churchy" as an adjective to describe him was closest to the truth,' she says. 'It left the exact nature of belief out of the conversation, while crediting his attraction to churches themselves. Often on excursions the key stopping-off point, if not destination, was some little church. The more obscure and neglected the better.'

'He had a marvellous eye for architectural detail.'

'Liked a graveyard too,' she said. 'I've spent many hours looking at stone.' She stares at the tea things with clear distaste and offers something to the vicar, who refuses, less it seems because he doesn't want to eat a piece of cake than because his hostess would plainly have struggled to serve him. She swallows hard, as if swallowing something down. 'Tom had made a small wooden spade and we carried this when we visited graveyards. It was to scrape the moss off so he could read names and dates. He had his own tool.'

'Ingenious.'

'Reverend, they talk of his magisterial position, his eminence, but not long ago, he said to me, "All I wanted, Flo, was to have some poems or a poem in a good anthology like the *Golden Treasury*."'

'The simplicity and the humility.'

'Another thing he liked saying, "I would have preferred to be a small architect in a country town."'

'The modesty.'

'May I quote something from his diary? I have it in my head for some reason. So many things, it turns out, are committed to memory without my even trying or knowing. This: "Coming back from Talbothays by West Stafford Cross I saw Orion upside down in a pool of water under an oak."'

The vicar nods thoughtfully.

'He saw large things,' she said. 'But then if he sat down for dinner and a lace doily had gone even a little awry, he would fix it.'

'Large and small.'

'He could drive the servants mad.'

'Exacting standards.'

'I feel crushed to the earth.'

'My dear Mrs Hardy.'

'I thought I was prepared but I wasn't.'

'Can anyone be prepared?'

The house shakes slightly. Another cattle-truck changes gear outside to take the hill.

She stands up and looks towards the sound. 'He wrote to the paper about those.'

'About?'

'Those trucks. He stood at the gate and saw the cows' heads pressed through the rails, their terrible eyes, tongues hanging out. He saw it and was sickened and angry. Shaking when he came inside, quite upset. The noise still horrified him. There were donkeys too.'

'Donkeys?'

'Never mind. These cattle-trucks, they drive at night so we won't see the animals but only imagine them.'

'He felt things,' says the vicar. 'The welfare of animals is a great test for me of a man's character. I've had many wonderful and enlightening conversations with Tom on the subject of cats. Hedgehogs too, I remember.'

'He liked to watch them from the window, yes. Owls too.' Mrs Florence waves the newspaper about. 'I hold it to my face if I need go out the door. The photographers won't leave. Wess has bitten two of them already but Nellie says now they carry packets of meat from the butcher's and the dog is quite theirs. Making him the only one eating much, I'm afraid. The house threatens to go to pieces.'

The vicar stands up and grips Mrs Florence's hands, just as he'd done with ours at the door.

'Tom didn't attend church, Reverend. It was a cause of great friction with the first Mrs Hardy. He upset her terribly with some things he said. She gave up reading his work too. Then when she died, all those poems in her memory! Evidently some of the great love poems of the age.

Woman much missed, how you call to me, call to me
Saying that now you are not as you were
When you had changed from the one who was all to me
But as at first, when our day was fair.'

He lets her hands go and takes a backward step, looking uncomfortable. 'Still, Mrs Hardy, I believe your husband had the gift of charity.'

She walks to the window, considering this last statement. 'Once he made a rabbit from a handkerchief when John Middleton Murry was here, with his little daughter. And he gave it to her. She sat on his knee.'

They stand in silence. The sudden, sharp sounds of a dog barking startle Reverend Cowley but Mrs Florence doesn't react at all. The dog begins to whimper. The vicar looks around as if waiting for something to be done about it. Then there's the sound of ferocious scratching at the door. Reverend Cowley takes a few steps away from it. 'Will he be admitted?'

'Who? Oh. Poor Wess, he looks and looks. We should stay quiet and soon he will try somewhere else. Tom used to give him lumps of wood to chew.'

The scratching continues for a few moments, then silence.

Let me ask you, Nellie, who are the best visitors we've had at Max Gate? Who are the ones we have most enjoyed and should welcome every time no matter if they arrive unannounced?

I'm not sure, sir.

But whom do you think?

There's been so many.

Yes.

But Mr Sassoon always seems a lively visitor, sir.

Sassoon? Indeed it's good to have young people about. Dear Sassoon. Yet my favourites are different.

Sir?

It's the kestrels and sparrowhawks, I think, the ground beetles and wild boar, and the fellows with striped heads. Inhabitants of all the nests, burrows, holes, paths. The moths, the ants. The bark of trees orange where they face away from the sun, as if rusting. The deer and the mole.

Wessex went with them on their regular walks on the heath but was always firmly discouraged from chasing anything.

The upland thorn, I love. The mushrooms. When I was a boy you'd hear a wasp called a wops. And what was a paddock? Long ago it was a toad or frog.

*

Alex sits at the kitchen table while our Alice washes spuds. By the stove there's a large pan containing two skinned things that he shot, leaping. The dirt rolls in the water. Cook is with Bert Stephens in his shed—she goes there to watch him smoke his pipe since her father had a pipe and it makes her happy.

'I wouldn't ask it, Alice. That you were there, what a reward.'

'I won't talk of it,' she says. 'The privacy of a man's last breath.'

'I was with my mother at her end. Peaceful.'

'Mr Hardy was too, I reckon. Afterwards wasn't so peaceful, which takes over in my mind, everyone running and shouting when we didn't mean to. But at the moment, yes.'

Alex stands up and walks over to the stove where he lifts the lid. 'Nice rabbit stew, is that? It was all right then, the moment?'

She picks at one bit in a potato. 'It was Miss Eva in the room itself.'

'Where were you?'

'In the little dressing room off the bedroom. I could hear it though.'

'You were close enough?'

'Eva was taking his pulse, as she did.'

'This is Eva Dugdale?' He takes out his notebook and pen from his coat pocket.

'And he says to her, "Eva, what is this?"'

'"Eva, what is this?"'

'That is the last thing he uttered ever. I don't think ye should know that, Mr Peters. Or put it anywhere for others to read.'

'You've told it before, haven't ye?'

'Miss Eva's told it, to Mrs Hardy and Mr Cockerell and Sir James. The man from the *Times* came.'

'Did he hear it?'

'I think not. Because they said she was not to say it in front of anyone and the man from the *Times* had only an interview with Mr Cockerell, which I attended part of as I did the tray. "Any last words from the great man?" says the *Times*, and Mr Cockerell shakes his head, "Only the pulse weakening and failing," he says.'

Alex smiles. '"Only the pulse weakening and failing." Mr Sydney Cockerell's last words.'

'Nellie said Mrs Florence was to ask Mr Cockerell to telephone you when it first happened. But the Cock went to the *Times*.'

'It's how he works, I'm afraid. In the pecking order, we're at the bottom.'

She scrubs hard. 'What do you think he saw?'

'Mr Hardy?'

'Must have seen something to ask it, "What is this?" Must have felt something. They say he didn't believe in God but he must have. Otherwise the question wouldn't be there in the end, would it, Mr Peters?'

'Don't know why you're calling me Mr Peters. It's Alex.'

'When he said "What is this?" he was seeing something. But what?'

'I believe he has the answer now, Alice.'

Alice goes to the pot and drops in a handful. 'After, Miss Eva was the one dressed him, and gave him a shave since that hadn't been done in a few days. She'd been experienced as a nurse. I said and what was that like? And she said it was a privilege. And I said but what did ye feel and she looked at me strangely, as if the question had never occurred to her. Finally she said, oh my hand shook a tiny bit, I had to steady it, and it was a time before she could get a proper stroke, afraid she was to wake him. Now he lies so handsomely in his scarlet university robe.'

'And about to be burnt to ashes.'

'No!'

'Consigned to a little pot and sent to London.'

'Please!'

'But it's what'll happen, Alice.'

She takes a fork and pushes a few potatoes under. 'Usually I'm not to say who comes and goes to the house, but Reverend Cowley visited.'

'He was here? And would you say it was a good visit?'

'Don't know. He doesn't like dogs though and Mrs Hardy said something to Cook on that, rather suggesting she had lost some of her good opinion on the man.'

'But they talked about the funeral?'

'Am I a spy in this house completely? I go about my jobs.'

'And I mine, Alice.'

'I heard nothing, only that Mrs Hardy was upset and quoting poetry.'

'Poetry?'

'Poetry that Mr Hardy had written to Emma Hardy, the first. Which if ye ask me may sway it away from Stinsford.'

'How so?'

'It's obvious! To give him to Stinsford is to allow him eternal rest in the arms of Emma. There's no love lost there. Old Florence cannot bear the thought. But anyway, ye must know all this from Nellie.'

'Some of it, though I've never heard it put like you just did.' The reporter places the end of his pen in his mouth. 'It's a point, isn't it, Alice.'

'For a woman to give over one's husband like that to a rival, I don't see it.'

'But of course the husband and the rival are both dead.'

'And I don't see that makes a difference.'

They both look into the pot, almost shoulder-to-shoulder.

He says: 'And how is Nellie? How is she coping?'

'Do ye think I'm the go-between, someone to carry messages?'

'No but I was hoping to call you a friend, and I know you're a friend of Nellie's.'

'Friends know when to keep out of things.'

'And when to help.'

She stirs the stew with a wide motion of her elbow, catching him and forcing him to take a step away. 'Find it hard to believe you'd be relying on me to help, Mr Peters.'

'Back to Mr Peters.'

'Call me Alice, then, though mostly that's because ye don't know and have never asked what my surname is.'

'Guilty as charged. May I now ask what thy full name is?'

'Why, so it goes in that little book with all the other names of girls you've met?'

'I'll remember it.'

'Will ye just. I'll test you on that when I see you again. If I see you again.'

'Go on then, I'm ready.'

'Are ye?'

'I am, I am. I swear it. So I'll know ye better, what's your last name?'

'It's Riglar.'

Alex stares at her, then they both burst out laughing.

'What is it?' he says.

'Riglar.'

'I am going to have to get my book out for the spelling.'

'You pig!'

'Because—' they're laughing hard now, 'because when I go fishing I sometimes use a fly called—'

'Stop it, you swine!'

'—a Little—'

'You!'

'Little Wriggler!'

She pushes him with both hands and he stumbles back against the door where Cook is entering. He avoids her just. Cook's cheeks are rosy from the cold. She carries a knife and the icy heads of two lettuces. 'If that fire dies,' she says, 'I'm holding both of you clowns responsible. A man's body lies upstairs and you two are having fun!'

'My fault, Cook,' says Alex. 'I promise we shall not have any more fun.'

Alice giggles.

'Shush, you silly girl,' says Cook. 'Go upstairs and see what needs doing.'

'Yes, Cook. Sorry, Cook.'

'Better yet, go outside and feed the birds. Has anyone fed the birds today? Is it that because Mr Hardy is no longer able to remind us we now forget ourselves and everything else into the bargain? Forget the poor birds struggling in the cold? You know how he hated anyone to say "What a lovely frosty day" when this so carelessly neglected the suffering such conditions brought to all the creatures. Go on now, girl, and at least pretend you have others in mind.'

The fire in F.'s bedroom is almost out when I enter and she's lying on her bed looking up at the ceiling. Her bedside light is on but the rest of the room is in near-darkness. I tell her it's very chilly and that I'll revive the fire, if that's all right. She doesn't like an over-warm bedroom to sleep in but she's lying down in her clothes and sleep doesn't look near. There's a murmur from her I take as assent and I shovel more coal on. I ask her if there's anything she needs. No, she says weakly. Would she like me to look in later, perhaps in an hour? I could bring her some tea. She tells me that would be most kind. I'm at the door when she pops upright.

'What's happening in the house, Nellie?' she says.

'Nothing,' I say. 'It's very quiet. Everything's under control.'

She swings her legs off the bed. 'So much to do. I thought of a million people I need to write to.' She moves to her desk and switches on the lamp. 'Did someone turn on *Children's Hour* for Wessie?'

'Alice turned on the wireless but he didn't seem interested.'

'Poor Wessie. I remember when we were at a dress rehearsal of *Tess* and he was a complete angel until it turned six and he realised he was missing *Children's Hour*. We had to take him home he howled so much. The actors thought it was the play upsetting him. Sir James was there.'

'He's sleeping on the hearthrug in Mr Hardy's room, ma'am.'

'I presume you mean Wessex and not Sir James, although I do like the image.'

'Sir James isn't in the house, ma'am.'

'No, he's out in the world doing his best for us.' Impossible to tell the tone of this. Did she even know how she felt at this moment?

'Cook was wondering if Sir James will be dining here tonight.'

'Best to have some things prepared, don't you think, Nellie? Some soup perhaps. And a pudding. At this stage things are fluid, and so the dinners should match.' The joking is accompanied by an odd shake of her shoulders.

'Yes ma'am.'

I ask her if she'd like a supper tray brought to her but she waves a hand to say she isn't hungry. 'Don't go,' she says. 'Tell me again what happened, where you were. You were in the dressing room.'

'No ma'am, that was Alice.'

'Of course it was Alice. Am I mad? I'm sorry Nellie. My mind's all in pieces, I'm afraid. And how is Alice?'

'She's okay, ma'am. Upset of course, we all are.'

'Of course, of course. When she's better I'd like to speak to her.'

'I'm sure that could happen any time you wish. Shall I ask her to come now?'

'No! I'm not ready now.' She's spoken fiercely and looks confused with herself. She sinks into the chair and rests her arms in front of her on the desk.

'I do want to say, ma'am, on my behalf and everyone's behalf, how sorry we are about Mr Hardy. Even though he lived a long life, it's still a huge loss, for you and for everyone who knew him.'

She turns to me and smiles. Her face is puffy and grey. 'Thank you, dear Nellie. Thank you.'

'And I would like to say that we are here to do everything we can to help you through this terrible time.'

'How awfully kind you all are, thank you.' She has tears in her eyes. Me as well. 'Awfully kind. And I must learn that the loss is only in a small way mine. As you rightly say, there are so so many who will be feeling deprived. Thank you for pointing out that even in this, my tendency for inwardness and miserliness is something to fight and overcome, if I can.'

'Ma'am, I didn't mean that.'

'No, but I see it nevertheless. I'm a wretched person, Nellie.'

'No, ma'am.'

'But you're too sweet to see.'

'I see a great deal of self-sacrifice.'

'Oh, that.' She turns to me, great grey rings under her eyes. 'Do you know a woman called Gertrude Bugler?'

I don't.

'A young woman whose chances I sabotaged for no reason but my jealousy.'

Where are the women to whom she might tell these things? There are none. Eva? No. For it was plain to see the helpless pride Eva carried in her sadness—that she'd had the last of T. H., the precious end; even blameless Eva couldn't help but communicate, wordlessly, a satisfaction denied her sister.

'She was an actress. Mr Hardy had known her family for years—the father is a confectioner in town, and he had a soft spot for her. Sweet on the confectioner's daughter! I am mad, the way these things tumble out! She'd auditioned for the part of Tess in the play—the same one I mentioned that Wessex had to leave in disgrace. But his disgrace was nothing compared to mine, since mine remains secret.'

Remains secret, she said. Noted. Because I was nothing— certainly not a teller of this.

She was speaking on.

'Tom had seen Gertrude in one of those dire local productions of his works they put on at the Corn Exchange and he was quite crazy about her. Oh, she was striking. Easily the best thing about the play. Everyone could see that. And he mentioned her to me frequently. He spoke to his friends about her. There was nothing hidden about his enthusiasm. As a topic, she was riveting to him.

'Then after she married I wrote her the most horrible letter, telling her she'd lost her refinement and fallen short of the standards we hold to at Max Gate. Whatever did I mean? It was wanton cruelty on my part. What was I trying to do except spoil a life? She wasn't a threat any longer, yet I pursued her with that mean vile letter. What must she have thought?

'Anyway, I believed her gone from our lives and then when I was home after my operation a few years later, I found Gertrude Bugler was acting again, in a local Tess. And more, that Tom was in seventh heaven. We went to see it. He was smitten all over. He spoke to me, very excited. I said things to him such as, isn't it possible to have too good a leading lady? Wasn't young Gertrude getting all the applause? Wasn't she unbalancing the play? Weren't the other members of the company getting upset at the attention she was being paid? But he couldn't see what I meant at all. And what did I mean? I only meant to ruin things. Plainly.

'He asked that a new illustrated Tess, then in the works, be based on the girl and he sent tickets so the artist could come all the way from London to see her perform. She is the living image, he said. And he made me write the letter of invitation, which I did of course. The artist came too—and cried at the performance.

'As if I was being goaded with a sharp stick, a whole series of wonderful opportunities fell in Gertrude's lap. She was offered the part with a professional company in London. Salaries were negotiated, dates fixed. A flurry of excitement. This was her dreamed-of break into the big time. Tom was a little worried now. Was his precious Gertrude ready? He came to me with his doubts. London was too much, wasn't it? How would she cope? Certainly he was afraid, but not for her I thought—for himself. How would he bear this loss? She was his creation after all. As we all were! He thought of us like this, I'm sure, as hardly alive unless he was there to watch us, to notice our moves, to guide us. Anyway, seeing this possibility of a break, I was extremely encouraging. Go, I told her, go to London and be wildly successful! Then I did the worst thing I have ever done.'

She was at the window now, the fingers of one hand spread on the glass. I had a sudden violent image of her placing her head through the glass. It hovered in my mind and left.

'I was ill but that is no excuse and I don't give it as one. I was ill, quite disorientated from the hospital, the operation. Driven by mindless fury at this pretty young girl's place in my husband's affections, I visited her house. I remember standing on her doorstep, ugly and hateful, and this beautiful creature, without guile, an innocent, with her lovely eyes, staring at me in utter confusion and fright, like a child told off for something she knows she didn't do. I told her there was a poem he'd written, a foolish doting old man's poem about eloping with her. I'd found it among his papers. He was living in a fantasy world. They would elope on Toller Down, where he believed his ancestors were from. He would follow her to London and then it would happen. I said that if she took the part on the London stage, he would set this mad thing in action and destroy himself, her, me and everything we'd built at Max Gate.

'I remember her nodding head and startled eyes. This insane figure on the doorstep, speaking to her from another world in some foreign language. And what did she do? She renounced the part. She lost her one chance. Gave it up because of what I said. She wrote to Tom giving some other excuse. It was the final communication between us. I'd told her I'd burnt the poem and I had.'

Unthinking I say, 'Was there a poem then?' Surely there wasn't.

She swivels towards me, ready to pounce. Horrified I've been listening. And now I'd spoken. As if her hairbrush had suddenly sprouted a mouth. Then she reconsiders. 'It's strange. I don't know. That's the honest answer. I really don't know if there was such a poem. The moment I said I'd burnt it, I believed that. The thing was gone. We were always burning things. I couldn't check that I hadn't imagined it. Do you see? There was an actual sensation of smoke in my nostrils with the mention of burning. I was unwell at the time. There were so many poems. I was on-guard for years. You can't guess how tiring that vigilance becomes. Emma Hardy was dead and I couldn't get at her but Gertrude Bugler was alive and living a couple of miles away. I struck without mercy and that thwarted life will be held against mine forever. Finally, I will answer for it, I'm sure. I'm as good as a murderer.'

It was absurd what she'd just said. It was demented, an irrational cry, with origins in distress and grief and incomprehension and—medication, that too. I knew it. I saw it all so clearly, the stricken, damaged look, the voice and mind strained beyond itself. Florence Hardy needed to sleep a long time and wake up and go for a walk. She loved to walk. Wessex would go with her, the usual route, and that pair would help each other. On reaching the seat where they normally rested, Wessex might approach and sniff it and would he jump up to sit beside her? Perhaps he would and she would let him—or maybe he'd take his usual post, staring out over the valley. I could reason it out, see the slow recuperation, imagine the path back. Yet I was rocked. And I was suddenly far along that path myself and it was dark, with the eyes of untold and unnameable animals and creatures on me, waiting for a stumble, some sign that they could—what? At that moment the air in the room, warmed by the fire, seemed fire itself. My cheeks were flushed, I thought. There was noise in my ears. I felt unsteady on my feet. My arms were heavy, my wrists hurt as if I'd been holding on to something for a long time. The woman in front of me was someone under a spell and I said to myself: here is the moment she will fly into a thousand pieces. Stand back! Shield your eyes! I felt myself cringing, preparing for it.

No memory of leaving the room.

I went to bed early, sick. In the kitchen with Cook I remember crying and telling her I felt sore everywhere. She told me I had a cold from all the foolish biking I'd been doing and sent me away. I saw Alice on the stairs and she asked me what was wrong and I cried again but told her not to touch me because I was probably infectious. The dog came out of Mr Hardy's bedroom and growled at us.

Fragment: a sweep has finished the chimneys and Wessex goes for him with great ferocity. He hated smooth-haired fox terriers because one had attacked him years before—one with a black face. And he hated black faces. Mr Hardy explaining all this to the boy after the attack, as if the sweep's to blame.

Terrible dreams of waking up in the tiny cavity of a hearth. Opening my eyes and seeing blackness, then at the very top of a long funnel (chimney?), a point of light. The top of a chimney above the roofline is called a tun. Then dust (soot?) falling into my eyes, blinding me. Ash in my mouth. Trying to call out. A talking hairbrush. The tangle of hairs vibrating.

Mr Cockerell was at the side-table in the living room, writing notes. Every few minutes he walked into the hallway and listened. If we were there, he'd ask us things. Is he come? What time was it? Was the train delayed? Then he went back inside. The fire dies and Alice gets it going again but he doesn't notice.

At once he stands, having heard the front door. The dog tears at the place he's now confined to. You can hear his paws. Cook opens the door a crack and throws him another bit of wood. He eats it like the fire eats it.

Barrie comes in a rush of cold, wearing a heavy coat and a scarf that he refuses to give Alice.

'Dear Barrie, welcome! You have the letter?'

Barrie hands him an envelope from the inside pocket of his coat.

Cockerell taps it. 'Dr Foxley Morris, Dean. This is a great victory! Ha ha! Tom in Westminster Abbey, can you believe it?'

'You make it sound like we've tricked them into it.'

'No! No, James! My God, you must be tired. Take your things off and warm yourself. How was the trip down? I'll get you a reviving tonic.' He goes to the drinks table and pours two whiskies.

'More of Tom's whisky?'

'Tomorrow I shall replace the bottle, if that satisfies your scruples!' He hands a glass to Barrie, who finally drinks. 'Aha! You're implicated now, Barrie!'

The Barrie slumps down in a chair, looking miserable. He's still in his coat and scarf. 'I tell you, I feel guilty enough.'

'Why? You've achieved it, you pulled it all together. A marvellous piece of persuasion and diplomacy. I knew you could. For me, it's a moment as if I were walking along one of these ancient paths round here and came across a Roman coin.'

'What do you mean? Got something for nothing?'

'Just the sense of history, Barrie! Don't you feel it? Like electricity! Things being connected up, which was Tom's message in his work—the cold, wonderful cosmos—though sometimes it can be warmed.' He taps the envelope again. 'Just in time too.'

'Why?'

'Reverend Cowley paid a visit from Stinsford parish. Upset Florence somewhat.'

'She's changed her mind?'

'She's confused. Poor dear Florence. Cowley will be working the family.'

'Actually I rang Kate and Henry, and Henry said basically nothing back to me when I was trying to arrange their travel to London, and when I asked to speak to Kate, he said she was in bed and unable to come to the telephone. Then he hung up.'

'They're upset.'

'They're upset with us, Sydney.'

'They'll come round. Just like Florence did and now,

under clerical pressure, always a temptation at these times, she has suffered a slight erosion.'

'A slight erosion? And the maids? Cook? Also eroding? The dog?'

'Basically,' said Cockerell, 'this is a house full of women and we needed to take charge.'

'Before I left, I don't even know whether Florence was able to take in what I was saying. Not properly. She was reading from his poetry. She was reading the things about Emma since I saw the place marked. Whether torturing herself or comforting, I don't know, and doubt whether she did either. I must see her.'

Barrie stands up.

'Not at once. Besides, it's late.' Cockerell is also on his feet.

'She won't be sleeping, if that's your worry. She doesn't anymore.'

'Dr Mann came again today and gave her further assistance.'

'Dr Mann came again and drugged her so the woman can hardly walk and talk.'

'Really, Barrie, I'm not sure where the source of all this agitation lies.'

'Nor am I, Sydney, nor am I.' Barrie goes to leave the room.

Cockerell says, 'One aspect I haven't managed to address with poor old Flo is the Hardy papers.'

Barrie turns and looks at him. 'Do you think this is the time?'

'Only I fear, given her state of mind and the terrific pressure she's under, that she might act rashly, feeling it was in the interests of the Hardy image, as we previously discussed. If the opportunity arose in the course of conversation…And one more thing, Barrie, a delicate thing I thought of.'

'What?'

'We put him in his Queen's College gown and we'll have Magdalene College there of course. Cambridge actually has precedence. They conferred the fellowship ahead of Oxford, any thoughts?'

'Are you serious? What does it matter? The gown goes into the flames. None of this matters anymore. Sydney, he's gone!'

One evening at the end of summer, my first at Max Gate, I was told to carry several wooden crates down to the back of the garden, where Bert Stephens had set a large fire of old branches. The crates were filled with papers: documents, letters, sealed envelopes, small journals, loose sheets of manuscript. I handed these to Bert and he placed them out of range of the flames. Traceries of sparks decorated the night air. The fire popped with small explosions and the tangy smoke made my eyes water. Bert poked importantly at the base of the fire with his rake, tidying the falling embers. Then without warning Mr Hardy was beside us.

He bent down to the crates and lifted a handful of papers. There was only the flaring light from the flames to see by, yet he seemed to be reading what was written on the first page. After a few moments, he looked up at the fizzing lines of burnt branches and, with a surprisingly firm movement of his arm, tossed the papers high into the fire. They fell among the branches, some catching in place, others tumbling down into the heart of the flames. One piece of paper lifted on a draft, alight, and floated away a few feet, landing on the grass on the opposite side of the fire.

'Get it, Bert,' said Mr Hardy. 'Quick now, man.'

And Bert stalked it down with his rake.

We stood there for another thirty minutes or more, while Mr Hardy fed all the papers into the fire. He always inspected carefully what he was about to burn. Sometimes I thought the look on his face, illuminated briefly, was sad; at other times he seemed very content. He always watched the material as it caught and burned. He never threw more on the fire until satisfied the last thing was done. Occasionally he asked Bert to use his rake to chase down something that had escaped on a current of air or to prod into the fire to separate papers that were burning in an unsatisfactory lump.

At one point he found items from the newspaper and brought them close to the flames. He began reading aloud: "'*Yorkshire Evening Post*, May 24 1895. Pearls seem to be the jewels of the season. The Duke of Aosta has engaged an English trainer to look after his horses. The New Zealand Parliament has, according to a recent calculation, passed in all 5,000 bills and repealed 4,500 of them. If this is correct 90 per cent of its work has been worse than useless. Mr Thomas Hardy, the novelist, is now in London." Am I, indeed? "Old newspapers sewn together and covered with turkey-red twill or cheap cretonne make very effective bedspreads." Who knew?' He looked up from the paper and then screwing it into a ball, tossed it on the fire.

Finally the crates were empty and he gestured to them with an open hand, waving his palm over them. What did that mean? He seemed desolate at this moment, though I couldn't be sure I wasn't inventing that mood. Apologetic? Contrite? Resentful even? Who knows? The effort of throwing seemed to have tired him dreadfully because he stumbled as he turned to leave, and Bert Stephens, dropping his rake, took him quickly by the arm and led him away.

The rake had fallen so the tines were touching the flames—I pulled the rake away.

I stood by the fire until I calculated the pair were at the house then I, too, went back inside. My uniform smelled of smoke and I had to hang it out the attic window.

They are in her bedroom, Florence sitting on the chair beside her bed, James standing in the far corner by the window. The coal in the fire pulses weakly like a lamp being turned on and off.

'I have some news,' he says.

'You've been successful,' she says, without looking at him. 'Are the reporters and people still outside the gate? They'll want pictures of you, you know. Famous visitor.'

'No. They've gone away for the night. It's late.'

'Is it? I'm just here, as you see. Wessie often wakes me now. Nightmares. The nightmare of a dog seems somehow worse than any of our own. Of course but for Wessex, I would have been alone on thousands of evenings, thousands. Tom was away a lot. I had a revolver in the drawer. Did I even know how to use it?'

'Florence, the Abbey says yes to the interment.'

She stands up. 'Would you like some supper? I could get them to do something.'

'No, thank you. Did you hear? Tom can go into the Abbey.'

'He would have smiled on that.'

'Would he have wanted it?'

'My dear James, his wants are now over. It's all us now.'

'But have we done the right thing?'

'Can you ask me that?'

'I'm sorry.'

'Can you ask me that, having already set so much in motion?'

'You're right.'

'To have second thoughts and bring them to me, at this hour.'

'I should leave.'

'No! Don't go! I couldn't bear that. Please. It's just my mind is so mixed up, James. His wants, his instructions, they're all mixed up. I'm not sure about anything anymore. On Boxing Day, his last one, he was in bed and asked me to bring paper and pen. He was so fatigued, I said we could do that later. Then he started outlining some changes he had in mind for his will.'

'You don't need to give me these details, Florence.'

'He told me he was considering an annuity to Kate and Henry instead of capital paid down. Which is probably to be preferred, don't you think?'

'I'm—'

'And the other alteration, again probably a good one, was to leave Sydney five hundred pounds instead of the percentage of his royalties.'

'I didn't know about the percentage.'

'A flat fee sounds better and the amount looked fair.'

'Perhaps your lawyer would be the person—'

'But, James, nothing was done! Tom was too weak to write, things got overlooked. I only thought of the conversation a day ago. Besides, Tom was drifting in and out of consciousness even as he said what he did about the alterations. Did he even mean what he said about Kate and Henry or about Sydney's share? I couldn't swear it.'

'Then you have a rationale for leaving things as they are. Probably in the scheme of things, such details don't matter.'

'You're right, yes. But what matters is my other thought.'

'What's that?'

'That I've made up everything I just told you.'

'Florence?'

'That I've projected my feelings about Tom's brother and sister and about Sydney onto Tom. Did the bedside Boxing Day scene even take place? If I can label Tom fatigued at that point, I remember how tired I was too. And isn't it too—too something—an old man changes his will in the hearing of his younger wife? Isn't it too much, James?'

'Florence—'

'Doesn't it bear the imprint of an impoverished imagination?'

'No, it does not. To be frank, it sounds exactly like Tom.'

'Really? I don't know anymore.' She reaches for a book

on her side-table. 'I was looking for things. Reading things.'

'I wish you wouldn't.'

'Never to hear his voice again, but we have his words at least.' She is flicking through the pages, trying to find it.

'Florence—'

'He wrote very little about me, for me. He'd finished with novel writing by the time I came along of course. Just the prefaces to the new editions.'

'Which you were a great help with. Indeed there must be a certain volume of—would there be?—of manuscripts and—'

She cuts him off. 'So I couldn't look for myself in the novels. But there are, as you know, these several hundred poems, four or five or more hundred poems, moments of thought and feeling, all conceived in this house. He wrote of the Titanic and Lizbie Browne, the gamekeeper's daughter he was in love with as a boy. He wrote about the dewfall hawk. He wrote about hedgehogs, insects, the plants. The trees inspired him. The upland thorn. But for me, virtually nothing.'

He steps towards her. 'You were too important to him.'

'Oh! Too important to touch with his art? I think you patronise me, James, a little. He was a reckless person in his writing, unable to contain himself. Many's the time that I called on Sydney to be my ally and ask, beg Tom, not to include certain things. No, I'm not there because of what I was to him. I think I had a significance but not a great one. He noticed if I wasn't there, I'm sure. He registered that absence. But noticing it, he did not long to have it filled again.'

'I think you're wrong.'

'I think you do not care to look too deeply, James. It is part of your appeal. Oh, I'm sorry! I don't know why I say such things!'

'No. No, I must concede that—'

'I only meant your intelligence was of such substance that touches on things gently, leaving in place what it uses. The gift is for non-disturbance. I treasure it.' She turns away from him. 'But I'm afraid I was a part of the house, like Cook, like Nellie, like Eva, in whose presence dear Tom was happy enough to die. No, don't speak! I think any one of us might have done that for him, and it happened to be Eva. Who else was close? Alice! Alice, the little maid, who was re-hanging one of his jackets she'd repaired the stitching on. She happened to be in his dressing room and heard it all. That evening he'd asked for something from the *Omar Khayyam*, and he might have died then, with me at his side, reading to him. But he did not. It was Eva, my dearest sister, taking his pulse, it was her arm he gripped. With a maid listening in the next room.'

'Florence, you ascribe choice to a circumstance in which I believe there is little or none.'

'None of us know that. None of us. All we know, as Thomas Hardy wrote, is the "infinite passion, and the pain/Of finite hearts that yearn". Finite hearts that yearn, James.' She puts the book down firmly on the table and rests her weight through her arm on the table. 'I shall destroy anything that is upsetting. No one shall see it.'

'My dear, tell me you'll think carefully first. The world may want to—'

'The world may want to what? Delight in our little miseries? Find comfort in our private pains?' She faces him once more. 'Emma told me once that when he was in London, she entered his study and sat in his chair. Tom never let anyone be at his desk. "I sat in his chair," she said, "and touched his things." And when she spoke she had such a fierce look in her eye, such pleasure and hatred.'

'Emma was, from time to time, unhinged.'

'I thought so at the time, and pitied him for that burden. I do not find the same response in myself now. What contradictions lie in another's heart, I won't judge. When she was dying, he carried on writing, told the maid her collar was crooked.'

They both watch the window, from which nothing can be seen except the confused reflections of themselves, the objects in the room. They can hear growling, then cats in a fight. Quickly nothing.

She says, 'Animals, it turns out, are rather easier to love. When I was first here, I saw the great disharmony. I saw Emma and her cats and thought her——. I feel closer to her now. How strange she was, how marvellous! Did Tom ever tell you about Yeats coming to give him the gold medal?'

'Of course I knew of it. A proud day, and overdue.'

'There was someone else from the Royal Society of Literature too. Mr Newbolt—didn't think I knew the name! We had tea together. I was invited. Perhaps to take notes? The two distinguished guests sat there and we all listened as Emma gave them, in great detail, the interminable stories of her various cats, several of whom sat on and around her. Mr Yeats in particular was involved in this conversation and seemed actually to be enjoying it. Tom meanwhile, whose day it was, continued to sink further and further into his chair, until he seemed hardly there. Finally, Mr Newbolt announced that it was time for the medal to be awarded and that Mr Yeats had a speech to deliver. Both men stood up, and Tom followed, while Emma, draped in and weighed down by her cats as if by a tangle of furs, continued sitting.

'Tom looked at her ferociously, as if to say: who are you and why are you here? It was a sentiment I must confess I shared. I felt completely his shame and embarrassment. She was dishevelled, her hair was a mess, and she'd prattled on to William Butler Yeats about her pets! "My dear, you must leave us now," he told her.

'The men heard this and immediately said that Mrs Hardy could stay. Everyone could stay, said Yeats, since the ceremony was an informal one and an audience, any audience, was better than none.

'But Tom continued to stare at his wife. No, he said, no, she would be leaving the room now since Emma had other business to attend to.

'Such was his tone, she did begin to make motions as if to get up. Two of the cats slipped from her lap and walked to the door, where I let them out.

'Yeats pressed further and urged Emma to remain where she was. The awarding of the medal would take only a few minutes and his speech wasn't one of those boring and interminable jobs—he saved those for London. You could see his discomfort.

'Again Tom said she would leave. He now stood over her. I saw he was shaking.

'Slowly, Emma got to her feet. Cats tumbled from her. She was old by then and suffered from arthritis. We all watched as she gathered her possessions and left the room.

I followed her out and closed the door behind us.

'He never spoke to me or anyone in my company about the medal. He closed it up in a drawer. When I'm being generous I think this is because he understood how poorly he'd treated his wife and how the medal commemorated that rather than literary achievement and he was ashamed of himself. When I'm in the opposite frame of mind, I'm inclined to think Tom always thought she'd ruined it for him, plain and simple. That she was there to destroy him. That the medal in fact belonged to her and had been awarded for long service in the erosion of talent. But let me say this, following Emma away from that scene, watching her slowly climb the stairs—it will always haunt me. There were cats waiting for her on the steps above and she said, "I'm coming dears, your mother is coming."'

Barrie clears his throat with a cough. 'I understand the vicar was here.'

'That man would consent to the Devil himself being buried in his churchyard if it meant more visitors to Stinsford!'

'So you think the Abbey the right place?'

For a moment it's as if she'll throw herself on the bed. She seems to look at it with this in mind. It's him moving which prevents any action. He goes to her. He takes her hands in his.

'Dearest Florence.'

'James.' She stares at their joined hands. 'The vicar stood as you do now, holding my hand.'

He looks at their joined hands, unsure. And she draws away.

'Once Tom told me,' she says, 'from within a period

of great despondency, that if anything happened to me, he would go out and drown himself, which, considered correctly, is a compliment, isn't it? Many similar vows have no doubt been aimed at yourself.'

'I hardly believe—'

'I cannot sign the paper. I cannot let my husband's will be overruled. I cannot go against the wishes of his family and of his district and of his soul. I cannot.' She walks again to the window and this time presses her face to the glass, cupping her hands, looking into the night. There is snow on the ground and everywhere though she can't see it.

The Barrie is rigid. He touches his pocket, looking for his cigarettes. 'I admire that,' he says finally. 'I admire your loyalty.'

'It was the basis of Tom's esteem for me, that I stayed by his side.' She draws back from the window and they take a few steps towards each other.

'A powerful bond,' he says. 'And what I detest is those who from a failure of imagination would lampoon it as servitude.'

'I was not his slave.'

'You were…soldiers together.' He takes her hands in his again. 'I understand that. It makes me think of—'

'It did sometimes feel like we were fighting an enemy! People always wanted so much of him and I had to stand guard. I know there are some who don't understand that about my role and consider me callous, as if I were keeping him for myself and preventing him from living the life he wanted. As if I had that power! And people would stoop to the lowest means just to get inside this place. Remember the time Tom believed Herbert Spencer had called and was waiting in the drawing-room for him but when he entered a complete stranger was there! "But how did you come by Mr Spencer's card?" said Tom and the man said, "Oh I picked it up somewhere." Then this devious chap wanted to go on with the meeting! I had to protect him, James!'

He presses her hands. 'Tom was forever grateful for your vigilance and care.'

'It wasn't just me alone in the battle against the world,' she says. 'In our allies we were supremely fortunate.'

How long did they stand together like this? All the clocks were ticking though the sound couldn't be heard upstairs in her bedroom. It was one of the things she liked about closing her door.

'But who were you thinking of?' she says. 'You were about to say—'

'Oh, the boys.'

'Yes.'

'Michael especially.'

'Oh, dear James.'

Barrie's tragedies, T. H. called them.

'I remember the year after Michael drowned, it was the day before the first anniversary, and that date loomed, as it always looms. I was thinking to myself, today Michael is at Oxford in his rooms and tomorrow he is going out to be drowned and he doesn't know it. Florence, I'm sorry, this is inappropriate.'

'No, please. You've never spoken about this to me. Please. He was as a son to you.'

'And I would have this dream, a recurring dream.' He is silent and turns from her.

She touches his back. 'If you can bear it.'

158

He begins again, turned away still. 'Michael comes to me, not knowing he'd drowned, and then as the day draws closer, in the dream this is, he grows sadder and sadder but doesn't know why. Yet I know. And it's my task, I think, to keep it from him. If I can just keep it from him. But he looks at me, he stares and stares, and I know he's in this bind—he feels something terrible is coming but what? Why this terrible feeling?'

She has put the knuckle of her index finger in her mouth.

He turns back and his voice is demanding suddenly. 'Do you think I should tell him?'

'But—'

'What would he want? To know? Do you think that would be best?'

'It's impossible,' she says.

'Absolutely impossible! So why does he come?'

'Because you were so dear to him.'

'I wake up and the sheets are soaked. Sometimes I find myself sitting in a chair, looking back into the bed, expecting to see myself sleeping but where am I? There's a sharp moment of utter panic. What have they done with me? Then I realise the real me is the one sitting in the chair.'

'You've suffered.'

He rubs his face. 'My deepest apologies, Florence. I must be so tired to have said all that. Forgive me, do.'

'Forgive what? The expression of feelings? The gift of that? This house has been too long starved of that kind of generosity. Tom was—'

'Tom had his own way of expressing things.' He walks

159

across the room to look into the fire. 'I remember coming here once and we went off to Bockhampton. Tom wanted me to see his birthplace. He wanted me to. And it was a lovely walk, really it was. And there was the cottage. Very charming indeed!'

'Oh well, yes, Bockhampton.'

'Florence, it was so charming. And he pointed out his bedroom, up on the second storey. The place was closed. But he said to me, "There, Barrie, in the grass, get the ladder." And there was a half-rotten ladder, don't know how long it'd been lying there. So I got the ladder and he directed me to position it under the window. "Go on up, Barrie," he said. "That's the one." Pretty much he ordered me to climb this rotten ladder so I could peer into his boyhood bedroom!'

'You should have refused.'

'But how? How could one refuse? One couldn't refuse. Thomas Hardy had produced a ladder and told me where to look. "See?" he called up. And I said, "I see, I see." I could feel the rungs under my feet. At any moment the whole thing might have collapsed. And he said, "That is where I slept as a boy." "Amazing," I told him. And it was! It was, Florence. Since that was the way Tom did things and we wouldn't have wanted it any different. He pointed to the ladder and told us to climb up. He had that power.'

Then there is the sound of raised voices and loud footsteps. A knock on the door. It's Sydney.

'Barrie? Are you free?'

'Sydney, open the door!' she says. 'What's happened?'

The door opens. 'Nothing's happened,' says Sydney.

'Because it's happened already,' she tells him. 'Nothing can happen anymore.'

'Absolutely,' says Sydney. 'Yet I do require Sir James for a few moments.'

'Here he is,' she says.

'I'm here.'

'Then shall we?' says Sydney.

'But of course,' says Barrie.

'There are so many things to take care of and our task, my dear Florence, is to relieve you of as many as we can.'

'But it's late,' she says.

'All the more reason for you to rest now.'

'Don't lock me up here, Sydney!'

The Barrie takes her hand. 'I'll return soon, I promise.'

Wessex runs past them and jumps onto the bed to bite the pillow.

The horse stood breathing heavily, steaming in the cold night, its load stopped behind, a cart carrying the body, a pile of blankets. Sweat smoked off its flanks. The men and our Alice gathered around it, their torches throwing beams of light into the frozen trees.

Anything chained, caged, yoked, driven, abused, toyed with, removed from its context, he couldn't bear. The country fairs finally were given up as too great a trial. That his dear father, without a thought, could throw a stone and kill a bird in front of him, presented an idea about human capacity he wished away but saw again and again. How does the sheep feel in its pen?

He asked passengers to step down from horses that were tiring.

One day he came to us in the kitchen and said, 'Here is a job I would like you to do, to share.' He was carrying a cat. 'Would you hold her? Today she has suffered a great blow, her kittens taken away from her. Hold her through the day. That would comfort her and me.'

On the road, Dr Mann is checking under the blankets while Alice sobs. Cockerell grabs Alex by the collar. 'My God, I'll have the police here!'

'Where is the poem of Tom's that calls us "human jam",' says Sir James sadly.

'I'd make it of this fellow! The thieving of corpses!'

'Look to yourself, Mr Cockerell,' says Alex. 'I was just returning this one to its rightful home.'

'Don't gloss the crime, Peters. The worst is that innocent girl you've persuaded to effect your grisliness.'

'I take that as my fault, that she's been caught, but not that anything wrong has occurred.'

'What did you hope for? To dig yourselves through the winter ground and roll him in like a frost-bitten turnip?' He lets go of Alex, aiming the torch once more at the glistening road.

Alex straightens his clothes. 'This is the way to Stinsford, where preparations have been made.'

'What preparations?' says Barrie.

'Come with us a mile and you'll see. We have the support and Reverend Cowley won't refuse.'

Cockerell laughs. 'Reverend Cowley, woken in the middle of the night, prodded on by an illiterate mob, to say a prayer for a body in a blanket! I didn't take you for a fantasist of this size, Peters.'

'Realist, sir. Literate, sir.'

'Barrie, I say we hand them over to the constabulary.' Dr Mann comes forward.

'How is he, Doctor?' says Barrie.

'My guess,' says Alex, 'is he's still dead.'

'There's no…damage to the body that I can see.'

'We carried him careful,' says Alice.

The doctor turns to her. 'You should not have moved him at all.'

'Oh, yes, Doctor, I see it,' she says. 'But don't feel it.'

'Don't feel it?' says Cockerell. 'How about the loss of your position at Max Gate? Would you feel that, Alice? The exchange of your current position for that of inmate at Dorset County Jail? Would that penetrate?'

'I'm sunk, I know I am. But I did right by Mr Hardy. What else could we two poor lammigers do?'

'The continuing claims for legitimacy here are almost too much! The attempt is to convert it all to a comedy when the fact of a man's dignity is at issue. Thomas Hardy lies on a cart!'

'I tried to get my uncle's car but it's in for repairs,' said Alex.

'Repairs?' said Cockerell. 'I'm lost, I am.' He turns to Barrie. 'Tom's due at Westminster Abbey in three days!'

'I know,' says Barrie.

'What shall we do?'

The horse shivers and breathes, twisting its head and settling.

Barrie speaks quietly. 'Let them go.'

'Barrie?'

The doctor is nodding. 'I agree.'

'You agree with what?' says Cockerell.

'To letting them go, Mr Cockerell. And taking the body back to Max Gate. And phoning the vicar at Stinsford.'

'My God, it's a lonely vigil at reason's side.'

'Is that where you think you are?' says Barrie. 'On the side of reason?'

'The principles of justice in which I was brought up suggest a wrong needs righting.'

'Seems to me, Sydney, none of this can be forced into harmony with principles in which any of us were brought up. Neither the actions of these admirers—'

'Admirers!'

'—nor our own actions—'

'In apprehending them?'

'In driving them to it.'

Mr Cockerell claps his hands. 'So this is our doing?'

'Whatever the swerve of cause and effect, there are facts looking at us.'

'I see the facts plainly.'

'One you don't,' says Barrie. 'Florence will not sign for the Abbey.'

'Come to her senses at last, has she?' says Alex.

'But—but she agreed,' says Cockerell.

'She was in a fog,' says Barrie.

'The fog has cleared!' says Alex.

'Not by much. But she spoke to me tonight and she is firm.'

Cockerell steps away a few paces, looks in the direction of the cart. He shakes his head and sucks in his bottom lip. 'Then these good folk should be on their way with the body of Thomas Hardy, with my apologies for the delay in departure. No doubt the gravedigger, risen from his sleep, rests on his spade, idle and dreaming of his bed. Better catch him before he tips into the hole. Go on now!'

'I'm not saying that,' says Barrie.

Alex put himself directly in front of the Sprite. 'You said to let us go.'

'You said it, Barrie,' says Cockerell.

'I'm not saying to take the body.' He shines his torch briefly at the cart. 'Florence had no hand in this. And best she continues to know nothing of it. Nothing. Is that clear? No one tells Florence Hardy.'

Alice says, 'She won't hear a word from me.'

'But what are you suggesting?' says Alex.

'Indeed,' says Cockerell. 'What's the plan, Barrie?'

'I don't know!'

'The facts look at you and you don't know,' says Cockerell. 'Meanwhile in London, the Prime Minister waits.'

'I don't care about the Prime Minister! And I wonder if this whole business with the Abbey is for your own glorification, Sydney! Your attachment to the Hardy name a way of—self-promotion, and whether for a moment you've considered what others might feel. My God there's a calculation and a heartlessness in you that makes me wonder how ever you came to be so involved in that household of simple people.'

Cockerell lets out a choking sound. 'Simple people? My dear James, you believe that even less than I do. Simple people? Tom and Florence?'

'He kept you on for your worldliness, your usefulness.'

'The man on that cart knew more about the world than anyone, knew and cared more. Cared about his reputation, cared about his reviews, cared about gossip, cared about image. Do you know what he did when he heard Yeats had won the Nobel Prize? Do you think he toasted literature? Do you know, dear good Barrie, what Tom did? Will you guess? He went to his room and wept like a baby. Florence let me know that. And then he was in a foul mood for a week!

'He may have loved all the little animals and preached loving kindness and no doubt there's a large bequest in his will for the RSPCA, he told me of it. But we also have the last things he wrote! What are they? An elegy or two? A personal lyric taking in the wonders of the natural world? A touching piece of nostalgia? The meditative wisdom of a man facing the darkness? No. Doggerel, satire against two other writers who'd caused offence by not loving him sufficiently.

'Is it offensive to say that I regard such an appetite as invigorating?

'I have no illusions about why he "kept me on", as you call it. And you're right. I gave him access to a part of the world he desired.

'The first day I came to Max Gate, I walked out with the manuscript of *Jude* for the Fitzwilliam—not because Tom was innocent but because he was knowing. He saw in me a use for himself. We were all that to him. Useful, or not. All harnessed to that…cart! The doctor, who helped him stay in the world. The district, whose world he plundered. Even you, Barrie. Sir James Barrie. And we accepted it. But I truly believe that in return I gave him no illusions about why I agreed to my place in the household. I thought him a great man.

'Did I love him? I'm not sure I did. I believe that was the job of others. But I loved his greatness as an artist and wanted to be close to that, and did what I could with my worldliness to ensure others saw it.' He gestures towards the cart. 'This as an ending to all that largeness feels like a sorry diminishment.

'I'm cold now, like the maid here, and I shall walk her home.'

'I know the way,' says Alice.

'Of course you do, dear,' says Cockerell.

They all look towards the horse, who moves his head as if to say, what is expected of me now?

'Wait,' says Dr Mann. 'I have what may be a solution.'

How they all came to this moment, I still don't understand. The house was full as they achieved the removal of the body. Cockerell was in the living room. I was in the attic room. The Barrie and F. upstairs only a few yards from the scene. And Wessex? Would he have slept through it? Yet they managed to pull it off. Alex, let in by Alice, simply took the body on his shoulder, covered in a blanket, and walked out. Perhaps there was no great weight by then.

The doctor pulls a pamphlet from his coat pocket. 'It was Reverend Cowley who put the pamphlet my way some days ago. He has an interest in the field, as I do, and indeed Mr Hardy had.'

'What interest?' says Barrie.

'Related to antiquities. It may, in the circumstances, strike all as unusual and extreme.'

'All are by now well used to that state, Doctor,' says Cockerell.

'Still, it might be best perhaps to first meet the proposition in print since that may shield one from initial feelings that could be unfavourable. I give this to Sir James.'

He hands over the paper and Barrie starts to read it, with Cockerell nearby giving him the light from his lamp.

'Well?' says Cockerell.

'I don't trust it,' says Alex.

'Is this what says what'll happen?' says Alice.

The doctor moves to Barrie's elbow. 'I should say, Sir James, that both Mr Hardy's siblings have seen this same information today. Henry and Kate.'

'But it's hideous.'

'I agree it's unusual.'

'And what was their response?'

'I can't say there was not disturbance at first.'

'I can imagine! And then?'

'A curiosity that shaded into acceptance, limited initially but growing in force. They don't object.'

'I'm astonished. And they would take it to Florence?'

'They would support someone taking it to her.'

'Cowley gave you this, you say?'

'A pragmatist.'

'Opportunist!' says Cockerell. 'Though I must say the coded exchange is very trying and I am even colder than before.'

Barrie passes the pamphlet to him.

'I thought I would be next,' says Alex.

The doctor turns to him. 'Mr Peters, Mr Cockerell is right in asking for the police to be called. As a doctor, I break my oath in not making that call myself and at once. It is only the reputation of the Hardys, and I mean the Hardys from all the generations, whose name and example you claim for yourself as representative of the county, which prevents me. I ask for your patience.'

Alex shrugs.

'I will go to Max Gate now,' says the doctor, 'and settle Mrs Hardy for the night, so that when you return with Mr Hardy, there'll be no issue.'

'Thank you,' says Barrie.

'You'll dope her till she agrees with what ye want!' says Alice.

The doctor stares at her. 'I give my word that nothing will be decided until Mrs Hardy is clear of mind. Anything else would be abhorrent to me.'

'Ab—what?' says Alice.

'Ab—,' begins the doctor, but leaves off, turning again in the direction of the horse and Hardy.

'As watching is best done invisibly,' says Alex, 'she usually carried a dark lantern in her hand, and every now and then turned on the light to examine nooks and corners with the coolness of a metropolitan policeman.'

'Not you with the police now,' says Alice.

'This coolness,' says Alex, 'may have owed its existence not so much to her fearlessness of expected danger as to her freedom from the suspicion of any; her worst anticipated discovery being that a horse might not be well bedded, the fowls not all in, or a door not closed.'

'What are you saying now?' says Cockerell, stopping his reading. 'What's he saying about a door?'

'No doors here,' says Alice.

'Just remembering,' says Alex.

'I wish you wouldn't,' says Cockerell.

'He's quoting, I believe,' says Barrie.

'Not more quoting!' says Cockerell. 'It's quoting got us here! It's reading that damages us! Have it! Have it, man— more reading!' He shoves the pamphlet at Alex.

Alex bends his head into the pages. Then he stares at the other men, disbelieving.

'And do I die of suspense?' says Alice.

Alex offers her the pamphlet. She glances at it while it's still in his hand but doesn't take it.

'The light's poor,' she says. 'In a nutshell what does it say?'

Worms are moving the soil he's dug, watched by the sheep, crows. It's the gravedigger. He's in a hole by the Hardy plot. He looks up and sees the birds. He bends down, picks up a clod of earth, and throws it. The soil worms its way towards the edge of the hole, trickles back in over his boots. The crows have moved to the church roof. Rain, light. The clouds lit, then black. The poor sheep kneeling under the dripping trees. In the grass, the cat carrying the mouse, alive, in its mouth.

The blade that shaved him, the hairs of the shaving brush. What animal gave these hairs?

He pressed money at us. This is for your hat that was chewed, this is for your shoe. This is for the time you were bitten on the ankle when you ran to get me my walking-stick. Who knows what they're seeing when they feel that instinct to grab at us as though we were shadows passing across their world. We are their nightmares, are we?

We bring them the things for supper. The Cock has come again. We have polished his shoes.

'So good to see you eating properly again, Florence,' he says.

'Cook's a great bully. Besides, rabbit stew, it was Tom's favourite.'

'It's not the time probably,' he says, 'but the question of Tom's papers, Florence. I wondered if you'd had a chance?'

'What he looked for in the stew was the correct proportion of vegetables to meat, that was crucial. Too much of either could ruin it. Yet he did not like to think of meat, what it was. Emma's membership of the Anti-Vivisection League was a problem, since the printed material she left about carried illustrations that upset him badly.'

At once they are not hungry.

'Of course it's never the time, really,' he says.

'No.'

'Still, there will be a great deal of interest in whatever remains, in terms of correspondence, manuscripts, papers, and so forth.'

'Of course.'

'And at a certain point, decided by you of course, my dear Florence, we both should sit down and conduct an inventory. We should see what's there.'

'Mmn.'

'Since the value, historical and other, will be considerable, I dare say.'

They manage to resume eating.

'Last October,' she says, 'we had a strange visitor. A little Chinese man. We'd refused him when he'd written requesting a meeting and then one day he was at the door.'

'Bothersome,' says Sydney.

'Yu Shan Kuo. The name's stuck.'

'Fee Fi Fo.'

She gives him a stern look. 'He was a melancholy little fellow, large round Chinese face, but the profile was in some strange way exceedingly beautiful. The maid had left him on the doorstep.'

'What did he want?'

'To tell his story, I think. It was a ghastly tale. We all sat there as our visitor revealed the most extraordinary details of his family. Both his parents had died, leaving his older brother in charge. There was a sister who was betrothed to a man the brother didn't care for. The sister was found to be "in the same condition as Tess"—these were our visitor's exact words. Our Chinaman, then a boy of thirteen, was deputed to murder the infant when born: He sat upon it.'

'A cultural practice?'

'He killed a baby.'

'Extraordinary!'

'He gave us this information without modulating his voice. His English was hard to follow. He told us he'd studied at the Sorbonne. A strange detail. Then to save the honour of the family, the sister was invited to commit suicide. Her brother gave her opium in wine, which she drank then died.'

'What a cheery visit!'

'At this point in the story, our visitor broke down. He sobbed aloud and couldn't continue. But what were we to do? He was a stranger, uninvited, who'd deliberately gone against our wishes, and presented himself so that he could weep in front of us. Tom and I were paralysed. Yet the man's pain was so real, so harsh and I could see Tom was touched. Afterwards Tom told me he was moved when the

173

Chinaman produced a clean pocket handkerchief, neatly folded and proceeded to dry his eyes with it, without unfolding it. Something about that neat handkerchief penetrated Tom's heart. Yet it was at exactly this moment that I wondered: is he a very clever actor?'

'You saw through him.'

'I don't know if I was right. He told us that if people asked him if he had a sister, he said no. Because how could he tell them he'd murdered his sister. At which point I thought: remember the baby and why aren't you in jail? Yet Tom was speaking very quietly to him now and very kindly. The Chinaman said that having read *Tess* he realised that he should not have condemned his sister but reverenced her. Reverenced was his term. Again Tom seemed almost overcome. His own eyes glistened with tears. Both men were silent, shaken by these confessions. And then Yu Shan Kuo, if that was his real name, reached down and from a leather satchel, pulled out a newly bought edition of Tom's poems and, stroking its cover, asked if Tom could autograph it for him. Tom was in no state to refuse or make his usual apologies. He took the volume and wrote in it while the Chinaman looked on with that melancholy face of his. Once the business was done, the Chinaman checked the inscription, and then suggested that perhaps Tom could help him write the tragic story of his family's life. Here I stood up to indicate the meeting was over and quickly ushered the visitor from the room.'

'It was all a ruse!' says the Cockerell.

'I don't know,' she says. 'We can never know. The man was very convincing. But I do know that one's respect for anyone who asks for an autograph vanishes immediately.

That might be my prejudice but I feel it. I feel the weight of a suspicious doubting nature. I find I can trust no one.'

'Present company excepted, I hope.'

F. stares off. 'I feel it's a burden, Sydney,' she says. 'A curse always to be waiting for the moment people disappoint in this way. So tiring. James is due tomorrow, is that so?'

Sydney nods.

She puts down her spoon. 'With the…with the doctor.'

'Good man, very good man,' says Sydney.

Suddenly she pushes her chair out from the table and stands up. 'What on earth are we doing to him? Have we lost our minds?'

Cockerell stands up. F. starts to weep.

'My dear,' he says. He moves towards her but she runs off. He waits a moment, and then sits down again. He is eating when I come in again and asks for a little more bread to mop up the juices.

A rabbit contained in a hutch. A skylark in a cage. Hard for us even to look into the pretty garden pool where goldfish go in circles. The ghosts in horses' eyes.

I was working at the stove that day, when the Barrie entered. He was wearing strangely an apron. Nothing looks right.

'Nellie, we need a container,' he says. 'A tin of some kind, and a towel.'

I wasn't thinking. 'What for, sir? What size?'

'Not large.'

'I don't know what thing is large in your mind, sir.'

'A biscuit tin, and an oven cloth of some kind.'

I start to look around. 'If there's been a spillage, I can come.'

'No, no.'

I hand him a towel. 'I saw the doctor come in before.'

'Yes,' he says, 'it's for him.'

I find a tin. 'Oh my! I didn't think!'

'No need to worry, Nellie.'

'Oh my poor Mr Hardy!'

He takes the tin. 'Not at all. Not at all, don't you worry.'

I point at his apron.

He looks at it, as if he's almost forgotten he's wearing it. 'Yes.' He looks ashamed of this fact—the apron's spotlessness—and he hurries out. A dwarf in a fairy tale about a butcher.

The Barrie was pacing up and down in front of the window, smoking, hoping not to see on the bed where Dr Mann is bent over the body, using needle and thread—the shape of feet underneath the sheet.

The doctor speaks without looking up from his work. 'In the case of the artist, Sir James, which would you say is more important, the brain or the heart?'

'Sorry?'

'Forgive me, I don't mean to be facetious or flippant. I just wondered what your serious thoughts were. The brain or the heart?'

'I'm not…there are many clever artists, I suppose, who

fail to move us. Also many artists of great emotion whose work seems...intellectually thin.'

'Interesting. So you argue for a combination?'

Barrie catches sight of someone through the window and speaks as if to himself. 'Florence!' He ducks away quickly so as not to be seen. In doing so, he finds he gets an accidental view of the doctor at work. A flash of something, as if from the corner of your eye you see a fellow diner inspecting his meat by pressing on it with a fork. 'What's that? Oh, quite.'

Dr Mann looks up. 'And that was this great man's strength, his secret, I presume?'

Barrie sits down in a chair, his head turned away from the bed. He looks ill. The doctor glances up again and sees this.

'I'm sorry, Sir James. From here on, I can handle things perfectly well myself. If you would like to wait downstairs ...'

'No. No! To be here, it's...an honour, I think. I must be here. No.'

The doctor continues to stitch. 'My wife says I should sew my own buttons on.' Barrie shows no sign of having heard this. 'I must say, I'm still surprised to have this... opportunity. Mrs Hardy—'

'I think she saw how this might satisfy all parties,' says Barrie.

'What a great piece of persuasion though, to see things with such levelheadedness. Remarkable, I'd say.'

Barrie is on his feet again. 'But Doctor, what can I do? Tell me what I can do.'

The doctor studies him. 'Well, there is one thing, small thing.'

'Anything.'

'Silly really. But I have an itch.'

'A what?'

'An itch, Sir James. That I can't reach.'

'Oh.'

'On my left shoulder, in that region.'

'Yes. Of course.'

'The surgeon's curse. Sorry to ask.'

'Not at all.'

He walks over and hesitantly starts to move his fingers over the doctor's shoulder.

'Down a fraction, Sir James. Yes. And a bit harder, please. Yes, that's got it. That's it.'

Over the doctor's shoulder, Barrie makes himself glance quickly in the direction of the face of his friend, which— thank god—is covered.

We were put up ladders to clean in the porch and that's where the doctor and the Dwarf came as they were leaving Max Gate by the front steps, by the stone dog.

Dr Mann carries the thing that holds it. Mrs Florence comes from somewhere, with a sprig of camellia. She gasps.

The doctor nods. 'Good day, Mrs Hardy.'

'Hello, Doctor. I thought you'd be gone by now. Only you said an hour.'

'On our way, Mrs Hardy. There was more to do than …' He moves the tin behind his back, reverse prayer, though it's obvious.

Barrie points at the camellia. 'Lovely.'

'It's very early. I don't know why anything would flower now.'

'Very pretty,' says the doctor.

'Actually on my very first visit to Max Gate, I came with flowers, a foolish girl, in the thrall of an author, hoping for who knows what. Dried flowers then. And he took them and went to smell them before realising his error. I was mortified. But he simply laughed! I thought it was a wonderful thing, a gift, to offer that laugh in place of my …'

'We go eventually to Stinsford,' says Barrie.

'Yes,' she says.

'I shall come back. Sydney's in London.'

'Good.'

'And in the morning—'

'I'm sure you have it all worked out. For which I'm immensely grateful, to you both.'

The doctor gives a little bow. 'The operation, Mrs Hardy, was a success, it—'

'Quite, Doctor. Quite.'

'And it's my understanding,' says Barrie, 'that tomorrow's trip to Woking where we shall—'

'Precisely! If you would take care of that, I'm in your debt.'

The doctor bows again and moves off.

Most days, weeks, months you don't see, hear, smell, touch, notice spiders. Then one day she says, Those horrible things! I cannot bear them any longer! We are like those things. People will be coming soon, a stream of people and we must put on our best face and show them

179

we are capable of carrying on. It will be in the small things that we'll be judged. There is an old ladder. Once you climb up it you are invisible, as if in the clouds.

'I must apologise for the tin,' says Barrie.

'It's grotesque!' she says.

'I believed the doctor would come with a…receptacle.'

She turns from him. 'Truly, a horror! And Tom ripped apart, and us to sleep the night in the same house.'

'Again, I thought arrangements with the crematorium—'

'Would you stop!'

'Of course.'

'We have made him as he was before. If you were to go in, there'd be no change.'

'I can't go in there.'

'No, of course.'

They do not speak for a time. Above them we are working in the corners, in the clouds.

I didn't see him laid out, didn't want to. Was scared, yes. Better, I told Alice, to remember him alive, moving, present. That's Mr Hardy. Not all of it stopped. I didn't even like to see him in bed. Better to always have him in your mind upright, walking, bending to examine something moving in the grass. But, Alice said, isn't death part of life? No, I said, who told you that?

Finally F. faces him. 'James, the Woking crematorium, everything, I sometimes feel I should see the things I dread, would that not be better than what I imagine, to face it all, but I cannot. Tomorrow, for you to be my eyes and one day to tell me something of it…'

'Of course.'

180

'It is one of my greatest terrors that once this is all over, you shall find no reason to visit here.'

'I will always come here,' he says. 'For as long as I'm wanted.'

She smiles. 'You know the night Tom died, after he died, I had the strangest dream. I went into his bedroom to look at him but his bed was empty. I patted the sheets to feel him but there was nothing. I turned on the light and searched for his body. It was gone! And why were the blankets missing? I checked again. It was a little like your dream perhaps—of Michael. Yet not really painful. I walked out of the bedroom and in again, as if to trick whatever trick my mind was playing on me. But the scene was the same: the empty bed, the messy sheets, the missing blanket. Yet in the dream I felt oddly relieved. I wasn't afraid or upset. I was puzzled. But I also thought, good, someone has at least taken care of all that for me. That is one thing I won't have to worry about in the morning. It's done, settled. Good. And I went back to my bed and slept for hours, hundreds of hours it felt like.'

She looks at what she's carrying. She thrusts the sprig at him. 'Will you take this? For…Tom, I mean.' She is gesturing in the direction Dr Mann went. The Barrie takes the camellia and bows. She enters the house beside the ladder. He looks at what he's got, brings it to his nose, then leaves, the cold dog's paws stuck in the air. Our hands are full of wevet, tiny dried morsels.

*

He lights the altar candles, genuflects, and then walks to the side-door. At one point he stops and waits, and then he adjusts the position of a bucket catching the rain. Bats live up there.

The grave waits beside the pile of wormy earth. The soil is puddle, leaves, ice. The cat looks at itself, walks between the sheep. Crystals. Frozen milk.

The oil-headed otter looks like leather to the dreaming fox. Chase him into water! Look at yourself. You have two sets of eyes. Both of you.

The night before she goes up to London for the funeral, I'm with Mrs Florence in her room, helping pack her cases. She's soft, blurry, incapable of basic decisions about what to take and happy for me to make them. There are boxes at the back of her wardrobe which I open thinking they might contain shoes or boots. But they are full of books. She notices this and looks into the first box, bringing out a book and reading the title: 'The Book of Baby Pets.' I see that the author's name on the cover is hers. 'Yes,' she says, 'this was my last book.' She flicks through some pages showing drawings of rabbits, tortoises, goldfish. She stops at a page and reads: '"While Mrs Bunny is feeding her young, she should have, for herself, a good supply of green food, and now and then a warm mash of milk and barley meal." What sensible advice!'

I tell her I didn't know she was an author.

She laughs. 'Author? You're too sweet.' She flicks more pages. 'Don't say author until you've heard this. It's my entry for "Love Bird":

If you have not seen us, at sometime you will,
Perched close up together with bill against bill;
And on hearing our quaint little noises like kisses,
You'll say, "There are few prettier pictures than this is!"

Author? Oh, Nellie, why did no one stop me?' Another page: '"Should a strange Goldfish be put with others they will often hunt it to death." Cheery message for the children, isn't it.' She drops the book back into the box and opens another box. There are two stacks. 'And here are my first books. Haven't seen them for years. *The Book of Baby Beasts* and *The Book of Baby Birds.* Why would they show up now? These are rather lovely though. I mean, the illustrations.' She opens one and holds it out to me. 'E. J. Detmold was very distinguished as an artist. My contributions are negligible.'

The book is indeed exquisite. The pictures are watercolours, refined and detailed. A magpie sits on a branch. The feathers have an amazing sheen. The eye of the bird is alive, not a black button.

'When these were reissued a few years ago, they omitted the text altogether and the books stood perfectly as art books, free finally of my little stories and poems. I remember crying on seeing that. It was such a clear indication of the limit of my talent. I'd known it all along and was shocked to be affected still. I'm so vain.' She puts the book down again. 'I tried to write a play, and even a psychological novel. This was many years ago. And did you know that Emma Hardy also wrote a novel? I retyped it for her and sent it out to publishers. It was called "The Maid on the Shore". But no one wanted it. I presume it was not very good, yet typing it I thought it no worse than many things that were published, and besides I wanted so much to believe in the world of Max Gate as a glittering place of creativity, which it was. It was! So we forgot the novel but there were other writings. I was the one who encouraged Emma to finish her reminiscences. She'd kept a diary and had made several starts over the years to turn this into a proper book. She had lost heart and I told her, no, no, you must push on! There was so much of interest, I said. Her position had given her a range of experiences that the world could learn from and enjoy. I helped her and kept her at it, and it was published and I felt great satisfaction. I'm not sure what she felt exactly. By then, things were so difficult. Yet I was right to encourage her and I was right about the book's usefulness. It was in Emma Hardy's book that Tom found the inspiration and the stories for many of his great poems. One wonders what would have been produced had that little book not made it. For Tom, it was a treasury. Don't you think that's ironic, that I colluded in my own misery?'

There is a third box which I open—more books. F. has drifted away from the wardrobe and stands by the window.

'*In Lucy's Garden,*' I read from the cover.

'What's that?' she says, without turning.

I repeat the title.

She says, as if reciting: 'Lucy and Peter, two dear children, who play in the garden, who watch snails together and use a tree hollow for the post office, and watch the apples ripen. There are garden parties too. When the leaves fall, Lucy is upset, until her mother tells her about the spring that will come. I remember it so clearly! It was the same year Emma Hardy died. I received a telegram. I was at Weymouth and I rushed here. And I don't know how it was decided but I moved into the house right then, making myself a figure of resentment among the servants. Nothing was planned. Nothing was secretly in place. Nothing was anything. I simply moved in. There was no choice. No one chose. Did he choose that I should, or ask even? I don't think so. It happened. One minute I was writing in my parents' house. I was writing about two children and the seasons of a walled garden and the next…That day started as any other and ended as the greatest of my life, the most catastrophic. What happened to me? Within those twenty-four hours, I seemed to leap from youth—I was still quite young, Nellie—to dreary middle age. Yet it was what I longed for, to be here. We received a copy of the *Aberdeen Journal* in which was written, "The news of the marriage caused great surprise in Dorchester." I hid it from Tom.'

She crosses the room and takes the book from me. 'Will you have the book? Nellie, will you take a copy as a gift? I'm sure it carries all my faults. I'm sure. But still, would you take it from me, to remember me with?'

'I'm sure I won't have trouble remembering you, ma'am.'

'But take it anyway, would you. I'd like that.'

'I'm very pleased to take it as a gift. Thank you, ma'am.'

She presses the book into my hands. 'Good,' she says, smiling. 'And it's my hope that in looking at this book, you'll forget all the terrible things I've told you, all the shameful things, all the ungrateful things, all the unworthy things about my life and about the people in it and about Max Gate. I hope you'll replace all that with this simple, sentimental story about a girl in a garden. Because in my best moments, I believe in that. I see myself like that and consider myself, despite all that's happened, a lucky person.'

Where is that book now? Fuzzy feeling of looking for something in the garage. Stuff crashing around outside.

The Abbey animals with bulging eyes, wings, coming out the sides of the building, hundreds of feet above. God believes in them. Leaping stones.

The overgrown coffin covered with a white satin cloth. Pigeons flying outside. On the path, the broken bits of a crowshell, picked clean of its river-mussel.

The two men sit in a pew after the service, facing the front and not looking at each other.

'The rain didn't stop them all coming,' says Cockerell. 'I estimated thousands.'

'No, the rain was magnificent,' says Barrie.

'Hardyesque, someone said.'

'There was a queue at 10am. Germans, Swedes,

Frenchmen, Dutch. Turbanned Hindus! The world was waiting, Barrie! The world came today!'

'I saw a very unhappy G. B. S. just now.'

'What did he say?'

'Oh, that Kipling in front of him kept changing his step, thought he was going to fall over him and the entire thing collapse before they made the south transept.'

'I had Galsworthy in front of me. He tottered occasionally.'

'So pleased you were there as one of them, Barrie.'

'Honoured.'

'Shaw and Kipling had never met before!'

'One imagines the world smaller than it really is.'

Cockerell flexes the fingers of one hand. 'Today I thought it the perfect size.'

'Did Florence hold up?'

'Stood tall walking in.'

'Good,' says Barrie. 'Thank you.'

'Walking out, I felt her then on my arm.'

'Yes. Poor thing. She's straight for the train to Dorchester now. I think it's best.'

'Will you go down soon, Barrie?'

'She's asked.'

'Decent of you.' Cockerell looks across at a statue carrying a sword. 'I hope that soon we are to meet about the literary estate.'

'Good.'

'I think it will be a revelation. The notebooks and so on, the prospect of other work, unseen. It will build on what's happened here today.'

'Indeed.'

They sit in silence. Barrie is patting his pockets.

'I rather think, Barrie, we will have to wait until we're outside to smoke.'

'Force of habit.' He coughs suddenly, violently.

'Okay, old chap?'

'This chest.'

'Take care, you know. I don't want to press for another of these for a good while.'

'Relax, Sydney, I'm not a candidate for this place.'

'Don't speak too soon.'

Barrie coughs again. 'I remember Tom taking me to Stinsford.'

'Ah, yes, we all got the tour.'

'And he pointed out the family graves and Emma's of course and the space for Florence. He said he would be buried exactly between his two wives. Then he added that to be truthful on some days he decides it will be a few inches nearer to the first, on other days nearer to the second.'

'Yes! Yes, I understand that wandering measurement, I do!' says Mr Cockerell. He knocks the edge of his hat appreciatively against the pew. 'Shaw asked me what part of Hardy was it that you were all pretending to carry!'

'I had the Master of Magdalene come up, sweet old thing, kept talking about the purple carpet until I guessed. He was angling to know which gown Tom had been dressed in. Told him I didn't know.'

'I thought that might come up.'

'And you were right.' Barrie moves his leg as though it's become stiff. 'I must apologise, Sydney, for things I said.'

'Nonsense.'

'I said none of this matters.'

'And it doesn't.'

'You have my apology.'

'And you mine.' Cockerell adjusts his tie. 'At the end, what was it? The music.'

'From *Saul*,' says Barrie.

'Yes!'

'Beautiful.'

'Takes Handel to have the last word.'

'Did you think it all right? The whole thing. This. Alfred Noyes was at my elbow before. He's writing something for the *Guardian* which will be upsetting, I think.'

'Who will read it?' says Cockerell.

'True.'

'What was the tenor of it, the Noyes piece the nation is waiting on?'

'Oh, that Hardy's own sense of emptiness had chilled the whole ceremony. That the bleak drizzle was in harmony with the mental atmosphere. And that the sublimest words in the English language—"I am the resurrection and the life"—in their utter indifference to Hardy's own words conveyed something majestic on a ceremony that defied all logic.'

'Well, it's in the *Guardian*.'

There was at this moment a noise from somewhere in the Abbey, a chair fallen over, some piece of equipment, that echoed, and recriminating voices too, louder than the owners knew. A man and a younger person, whispering fiercely.

'Ever come across Clive Holland?' says Cockerell.

'The name is familiar.'

'Old friend of Tom's, used to go cycling and walking with him. Told me the most remarkable thing. They were on a walk above the Blackmore Vale, lonely stretch of road apparently. Between High Stoy and Bubb Down Hills, from which spot Tom was pointing out the ribbons of the English Channel and the Bristol Channel. Anyway, suddenly Tom asks, "If you had the chance to say whether you would be born would you have been born?" Poor old Clive Holland! So he says, "Yes, of course. Yes." And after a pause, Clive asks Tom, "What about you?" And Tom shoots back, "No, certainly not."'

The men sit in silence for several moments.

'You weren't troubled, Sydney? By all of this.'

'It's death, my friend. Naturally I'm troubled. But it's the complacency and smugness of people like Noyes which is offensive. Besides, Alfred Noyes will be forgotten—as I will be forgotten—no resurrection for us! Whereas this ceremony, despite all its awkwardness, elevates a deserving figure. Only a mean liturgical spirit would quibble over the terms of that honour.'

'Yet he never wished even to be born.'

The voices have gone. It has become utterly still.

'Now,' says Cockerell, 'we must remember about the fellow, the artist, who is keen to arrange a sitting with you all, the pallbearers and perhaps the PM.'

'For what?'

'The National Gallery, he says. A trial, I know. Though perhaps worth undergoing.'

'If you think so.'

'I do. The National Gallery. It is a rare moment in time, a rare gathering. Good to have it on the record. You were here, Barrie. You were part of it.'

'Aye,' says the Scottish Sprite.

Meanwhile at Stinsford, the other funeral service. The small full church is singing loudly, especially Alex. We hear him.

In the back row, a young boy is carving his name into the wood with his fingernail. His mother sees him and clips him over the ear hard, not missing a beat in her singing.

Here is the body of our friend.

Pain, nakedness. Faces of suffering, babies. Little animals crouching in the shadows. A dog on a chain, a bird in a cage. Light coming through the clouds like arrows. The blue windows.

They are now walking slowly towards the entrance of the Abbey, where Mr Thomas Hardy went before, over the grey sinking stones.

'By the way,' says Cockerell, 'in the line of Alfred Noyes, I'd avoid Gosse.'

'What is it?' says Barrie. 'Edmund can't have been expecting a pallbearer's position.'

'No. The thing at Stinsford. Calls it "medieval butchery". I've told him his view is his own and a public comment at this stage wouldn't be helpful.'

'I will never have that biscuit tin out of my head.'

'Dr Mann's pamphlet, what was it called?'

'"Heart Burials in Medieval Times", published in the *Field Club's Proceedings Journal* by G. Drury.'

'You have it well stored!'

'It's committed, for some reason. Perhaps because when I'm challenged on it, I'll at least sound scholarly and not like an utter ghoul.'

'Dr Mann, though, is a curious fellow all told.'

'Like many of us, Sydney, as if Hardy had invented us.'

They walk on, the light growing stronger, the wind catching their trouser legs.

'I make a confession now, Sir James, that may surprise— this is the place after all. I've not read any of the novels.'

'Hardy's? None?'

'Not one.'

Barrie is laughing softly. 'Not read a Hardy?'

'Never quite got around to it. The man himself seemed sufficient.'

'And it never came up between you?'

'Tom was good like that. And I feel as though I've read them. With people's quotations and so on.'

'Then here's another, to save you any further trouble. An episode from *The Woodlanders*, yes?'

'Of course the titles are familiar to me. *The Woodlanders*.'

'Good. Anyway, there's the death of an old woman reported in that book, and what the woman says about her impending doom. How after she's drawn her last breath, her relatives must get all her coffin clothes from her chest of drawers, a flannel to put under her and new stockings for her feet. She's prepared it all. And then she says there are four pennies in one of the drawers, two for her right eye and two for her left.'

'Tom would have heard the story somewhere. A local woman.'

'And when the pennies are in place, she says, and her eyes don't open no more, they are to bury the pennies with her. "Don't spend them," she says, "bury them with me." And then along comes Christopher Coney.'

'Who is Christopher Coney?'

'The local lad who knows about the pennies and who, one night, goes to the grave and digs them up and spends them!'

'What is this, Barrie, in the line of metaphor for what we've done? Taken Tom's pennies?'

'No, I just recalled the story. In fact I recalled it in the service, at the lesson, "Let us now praise famous men", and I heard that old woman, with her hopeful instructions, and I heard Thomas Hardy and thought of those pennies, dug up from the grave and put back into the currency of the world. And I thought maybe the boy, in his cunning, was the life force, moving everything back into the light.'

The men stand, looking up at the vast ceiling of creatures, darkness, faces. Finally, Barrie moves a few steps away. 'Will you come? There are people to see.'

'Soon.'

'You know, Sydney, I have a strange dread of this next period.'

'The crowds?'

'No, I mean after all this. I feel we have inherited a large enterprise and neither of us is quite prepared for it.'

Barrie touches the other man on the shoulder and walks out. Cockerell stays motionless. Anyone coming upon him in this pose might think of the devout.

Mr Hardy told us more than once about the canary that belonged to a neighbour, an old man, when he was a boy, and how if the canary was shown a picture of a cat, it would faint. He loved telling the story and he laughed every time.

Everyone else has gone and we should be too, only Alice and I have been helping with the dishes. Alex is there by the grave alone when we leave the church, posed in the bright cold sunshine under the great yew tree, a mound of dirt on the snow by his feet. Alice tugs my elbow. Since the body-stealing she's avoided Alex. Funny that. I tell her I'll catch her up.

'Didn't know you could sing,' I say.

'I like to sing. My mother sang.'

'You got it from her. Did your sister sing?' Remembering his nice tale for Mr Cockerell when they stood outside Max Gate in the cold.

'What sister?'

'Precisely.'

'Ah, you're too sharp, Nellie Titterington.'

'Oh, I'm a genius all right.'

He kicks at some snow. 'A good turn-out. I saw Henry Hardy. Did you see others from the family?'

'Some might have been distantly related.'

'Kate taken to London.'

'As help for Mrs Hardy.'

'So it might seem legitimate.'

'Mr Peters, do ye ever rest?'

'Mr Peters? Well, I suppose I deserve that. But I do find it hard to rest when there's wrong being done.'

'This wasn't wrong though. You agreed with it yourself, on the point of both you and that poor girl heading for the jail.'

'It's half right.'

'Heart right you mean.'

He laughs. A brief motion in the trees from the birds. Far off we can see the two old sheep that keep the place in order.

'Why would you do such a thing?' I say.

'I am sorry for dragging Alice into it.'

'You might have easily ruined her life.'

'It was a gamble.'

'To gamble on that!'

'I calculated the risk and I was right.'

'Ye were lucky.'

'I had to force the issue but I regret that I put her in that position. Not that it wasn't finally her choice.'

'You think she chose freely, in her state of confusion?'

He bends down to the snow on his haunches. 'You know it was your place she took though, don't ye?'

'My place?'

'I had no one else to turn to, Nell.'

'And ye think I would have been keen? You're that deluded to believe I would have agreed to such a thing?'

He stands up again, his head dropped. 'I was mad.'

'Ye were.'

'I was mad. I'd lost ye.'

'Oh, so this was all about me?'

'Had to do something to get your attention.'

'Very funny.'

He smiles. 'Did you see those four mourners in their red fox-hunting jackets?'

'I did.'

'I was about to go over and tell them to take them off. Did they know Thomas Hardy's opposition to the hunt? What were they thinking? Then I thought, no, let them be. It's a testament to the man that even people with such scant knowledge of his beliefs and probably his writings should be drawn to pay their respects.'

'People come to funerals for all sorts of reasons.'

'I suppose.' He looks me directly in the eye. 'What will you do now?'

'Nothing. My job.'

'She'll leave as soon as she can.'

'I haven't heard.'

'You haven't heard.'

'No. Nothing's been decided.'

He puts his gloved hands in his pockets. 'Did ye see who placed the wreath which said "the sorrowing woman"?'

'I saw her.' An attractive dark-haired woman, holding the hand of a young boy.

'That was the actress Gertrude Bugler.'

'I know the name.'

'A great favourite of Hardy's.' It was hard to tell if he was fishing—he was always fishing.

'Did ye write all these things down, the inscriptions on the wreaths, who was here and what they said, all of it?'

'Of course. It'll be in the paper tomorrow.'

'Everything for the paper.'

'Not everything, no. I can tell you one thing that won't be. But maybe you've heard about the doctor's cat?'

'What?'

'Dr Mann's cat, the doctor who performed the surgery on Mr Hardy's body.'

'Dr Mann I know, his cat I don't.'

'When they had the heart of Thomas Hardy in your biscuit tin.'

'I gave the towel from the kitchen for that. One of the odder moments at Max Gate.'

'They wrapped the heart in your towel inside the tin. I didn't know about your towel. I'm pleased to know that, Nellie.'

'Anyway.'

'Anyway. When Dr Mann had it, he took it home and the tin was sat on the doctor's mantelpiece. And the cat, what I've heard, stalks along and with its fine sense of smell—'

'You're making this up.'

'Walks along the mantelpiece and knocks the tin off.'

'This is good, go on. What a fairy story.'

'And with the force of the fall, the tin—'

'Yes of course.'

'The lid of the tin pops off.'

'The cat? The doctor's cat knocked the tin off? And who gave you the story? The cat?'

'Think it was from the doctor's girl.'

'I'll ask her myself.'

'You may ask, Nellie. This is what I heard. Do ye want to know more?'

'Go on. In too deep now.'

'Then the good doctor comes in to find the cat at it, with Thomas Hardy's heart.'

'At least ye never stop trying.'

'Not my words, Nellie. I work as a reporter. What I write must be verifiable.'

'You'll not write that though, will ye.'

'No, I won't. Because of feelings.'

'Right, feelings.'

'Because of, finally, the honour of what lies here and all about.'

'Naturally.'

'Some would say a story like that, if printed, would bring shame on us. I don't say shame is stopping me, Nellie.'

'No.'

'I say, there's truth.'

'Yes?'

'And there's compassionate truth.'

'Ah.'

'Shelter from the truth maybe, which sometimes is a greater truth. I wouldn't say to Mrs Hardy what I just said to you about the doctor's cat having a lick at old Tom's heart.'

'Oh go on, she'd enjoy it.'

'But you and I can face the truth.'

'Is that right?'

'We can, Nellie. You know it.'

He might have tried to take my arm at that moment.

'I don't know ye,' I said, stepping way.

'Nell, who is madder? Us or that lot up in London?'

I studied him hard. I took in his slight smile that didn't reveal his teeth. I wondered. Even then I was tempted. Who was he? What did he want that was to do with me? My feet were cold in my shoes. 'I don't know what you're capable of. I don't know ye.'

'Ye came today. If we'd not acted, there'd be none of this.'

'Please don't speak to me ever again.' I walked away, hurrying to catch up with Alice.

Alex Peters left Dorchester a short time later to take up a job on another paper in the north. I didn't enquire which one.

The curtains of his study are opened. May sunshine! It's Mrs Florence. There's a vase of roses on a table. They've come so early, and after such a hard winter! No one's ever seen them this early. She makes a few adjustments to the stems, then walks to the desk where she sits down to write. She uses the place now. A few things she won't change. The calendar he had in front of him, always opened to the day Emma Hardy died. No matter what she says to herself, she can't close that calendar.

'Dear Sydney, I write with the news you may already have guessed, though I hasten to add this must remain a secret between us, at least for a time. James and I are to be married. The interval of only these few months since Tom died will strike some as insufficient and unseemly. In this decision I take my courage from Tom himself, who believed conventions, especially in the matter of love, to be irrelevant and often ruinous. Dear James has been my rock throughout this time.

'Your own magnificence as literary co-executor I acknowledge freely and fully and will continue to do so. As you said to me, to sing the Hardy name is our duty and honour, and one that I share with you in great earnestness and in great joy. The union James and I seek will not alter in any way the terms or spirit under which you and I conduct that singing.

'I trust your absence from Max Gate over this little while is unconnected to any feelings you may have on this matter, or any other matter. I cannot pretend the circumstances surrounding Tom's funeral do not haunt me. But it is James's idea to put this behind us and not dwell on any lingering pain or regret. "Let's just forget about all that." Dear James! And when he says it, I do totally believe in its wisdom. Don't you? Anyway, my old friend, do come again to us when you are able.'

She looks down at the bottom desk drawer and slowly opens it. She takes out the battered shoebox she held before. She places it on the table and resumes.

'To return to matters of the literary estate, I realise you may never understand, much less endorse, my decision to destroy the bulk of Tom's personal diaries and notebooks. It was his express desire not to leave ephemera behind. Having gone against his wishes, or at least compromised them, in the matter of burial, I find I have little strength or inclination to repeat the indignity, even given the fine arguments mountable in that direction. Here you must take the word of a wife but also of a reader—nothing of high literary value went into those flames. Much of it was domestic, humble. Tom's chronicle of the years was marked by the necessary slapdash of everyday rather than the care and patience of art and by judgements that, ripped from context, might appear dubious, or harsh or even ill-considered. Did the world need to know that on this day thirty years ago Thomas Hardy went for a pleasant walk? Or that he was once in dispute with a supplier of brass fittings? What would any of us feel should he be in a similar position? Would you or I rush to open ourselves to the world's scrutiny? His private pen must stay private.

'This is not to say it wasn't immensely painful to see so much of Tom extinguished, and at several points I was in danger of entering the bonfire myself to retrieve something. I recall Tom suffering similarly on the occasions he burned old material. He would be withdrawn for days and quite out-of-sorts.

'If I say there are one or two notebooks yet to be destroyed, it's not to give you hope as an executor but simply to indicate the ghastly shock I feel at watching over the immolation of objects I associate with his dear hand, with his body and mind.

'However, one item remains which I did not destroy and will not destroy, nor did I pass it on for your notice. Possibly I did not throw it onto the bonfire since it had already undergone that transformation.'

The perfectly-made bed, the stilled objects: a stone water-jug, a neat pile of books on the side-table, an inkwell on the main desk beside a plaque, a violin case (cracked), the foxed map of somewhere in a gilt frame, his little black felt hat, and hanging from a hook on the back of the door, a heavy coat. I went back in one last time, without purpose or authority, while she was writing her letter. This was the coat he wore on his walks, his rides. And in its pocket, a funny shape of something. Was I looking for a souvenir? My hand was feeling inside.

I remember the plaque. It read: 'Write, and with mine eyes I'll drink the words.' Who will? He himself? Others? Who?

'You will be familiar with the reception of Tom's last novel, *Jude the Obscure*. I do not consider myself professionally qualified to judge it as a work of art. Suffice to say that as a common reader I found it supremely troubling and there are certain images I wished had never been planted in my mind. Yet isn't that the proof of its power? Anyway, you will remember the fuss. Booksellers sold it in brown paper bags. The book was not liked and among some it was hated with feelings of great intensity. Here was an opportunity, some saw, to destroy Hardy once and for all.

'Such hostility and vilification marked Tom. Famously it brought the end of his career as novelist. During that time he received many letters and communications of outrage. A few of these offered point-by-point rebuttals of what the sender saw as the book's, and Tom's, distorted and erroneous views on religion and education and marriage and love. Mistakenly, I think, he entered into unsatisfactory and painful dialogue with these correspondents. Many others simply damned him to hell. The latter he found quite cheery. He kept none of these documents.

'There exists, however, one reminder of the period. For years a box has sat in one of Tom's drawers. It contains ashes. I discovered the box one day a few years ago when we were looking for something else. At first I believed the ashes were of human origin or animal. It was an unpleasant find. Tom put me right. He was laughing as he told me.'

She gently lifts the thing out of the box. She puts her hand to her mouth when she sees the stuff, ashes.

'The box had been sent to him by an Australian reader of *Jude*. They were the ashes of his copy of the book. This reader had burnt the novel and then gone to the trouble of sending the remains all the way from Australia. I asked Tom why he'd kept such a thing. "Because," he told me in earnest now, "these are the ashes of my poor Jude."

'Dear Sydney, I find myself paralysed on this point. What should be done with the box? This small coffin. I await your guidance.'

She stands up and goes to the window. In the garden, two workmen have arrived. They carry large handsaws. For a moment she thinks of knocking and telling them to leave at once. Who are they?

'I must add, sadly, and therefore inappropriately, the news that Wessex died two weeks ago. He was thirteen years in age and had been poorly. There was swelling and paralysis. Two doctors came—for such a creature, human doctors were required, not vets—and they administered a kind of chloroform in his sleep so that he never woke up. He is buried in the garden, the place shortly to be marked with a headstone. With his usual thoroughness, Tom had designed the stone years before and had asked Grassby Stonemasons to do the work. The edges and back are to be left rough and the letters cut deep. Tom and I had agreed that the words on the stone should read "Faithful, Unflinching".

'Were you aware Tom kissed him goodnight every evening?

'And did you know that when Sir John Squire once visited us and observed Wessie up on his haunches listening to music on the radio, he said, "His bite is worse than his Bach." I remember that now.

'We are all distraught. As you know, he was as a child to us. Unteachable and irrepressible, Wessie was for Tom and me, a model for the instinctive life. Of course we also try to be rationalists at Max Gate and must find in a dog's death the simple turning of the years. But it was Eva, my selfless sister, who perhaps spoke our truest feelings when she said Wessex had died of a broken heart.'

She goes back to the table and picks up a newspaper clipping.

'I enclose a photograph of Wess and Tom that appeared in the local paper last week to mark the event. The reporter came to the house—I have never cared for the breed as you know but this one was new and young and sweet and rather puzzled by the whole business—and we sat for some time as he listened very patiently to my long—overlong!—and emotional talk about our beloved friend. So sad. But the photo is not at all sad and I am happy to see it. Tom looks every inch the author, gazing thoughtfully into the distance. Wessie, in his usual pose, is jumping—as if life were to be snatched, quick, before it goes.'

She puts down her pen suddenly and stares at what she's written, startled for a moment. Then she stands up slowly, looks around. At the window she adjusts the curtains.

The men have started to cut branches from the trees. A large one falls heavily to the ground and a thing, small and bushy, runs off in fright, welcomed in by the long bladey grass.

PART THREE

How do some survive and others are not here? Disjointed thoughts upon waking with the radio on. I don't try to organise them. Wessex the dog listened to the radio. *Children's Hour.* We have a child, Jenny, and she has a child, Benjamin. Train-lines closed. Roads closed. It's all happened and continues happening and it is astonishing. At Cobham Hall School for Girls in Kent, pupils woke in the night to the sound of shattering glass as trees crashed through their window. Nearly sixty years since Max Gate. It is believed that more than two hundred trees in the school grounds have been toppled by the winds. We live in a city with millions, yet the foxes have come back. Cubs, they look like. In the hedge, the mother's beaky face. They scream and fight. If we sit in the dark at night, they walk up to the windows and look in. 'We'—do I have to stop saying/thinking that? There will be lots of things like this—whatever we shared, won't make sense now. Is it tomorrow a man is coming to see what can be done about the foxes? Almost think: I must check with Robert; and then stop myself. *Robot.* Robot was what Benjamin called his grandfather.

Really I'd prefer not to get up.

If everyone in the house can get up but one can't—.

I didn't sleep much at all last night. It sounded as though people were being shot. Rifle shots through the park, I thought. London was at war. Certainly under attack. Winds of over 100 miles an hour. Power lost to whole districts. Reports coming in of six deaths and police fear this figure may rise. Trees hundreds of years old lie destroyed in parks throughout southern Britain. In my dreams, half-waking, I thought: who are they shooting? Is that why I've been thinking of Alex Peters? It was the branches of trees! Oh, so only trees.

Selfish but the idea of getting up and hearing about the storms bores me. Even the prospect of talking to our daughter on the phone, as I must do, and which I enjoy greatly, feels a bit wearying. This new external calamity, which will no doubt claim a lot of time and attention, feels extremely insignificant. At once: the families of the six people who have lost their lives—do I imagine they are a nothing? Someone is missing off the coast of somewhere—do I imagine that person and those waiting for news are beside the point? So get up, get up.

That was my last piece of work for the house called Max Gate, to carry her letter to Sydney Cockerell in my purse, drop it in the box by the train station. It was summer, a warm day. I decided to walk, though Mrs Florence offered me the taxi fare. Oh, it felt good to walk. Through the woods and across the heath, abandoning the road. A young woman. Remember us? Bluebells, primrose, wood anemone. Grasshoppers on the path, beautiful colours, things that fly. Bees. Two old horses ambling to the fence to nod their noses, show their teeth. Mither ho, I almost call. Mither ho. Had one of them been involved the night T. H.'s body was taken? Suddenly all that seemed very long ago, as cold weather is hard to remember. There were violets. I had to wear my winter coat because it wouldn't fit in the bag. My hat too. It was extremely hot in the trees. What a strange creature I must have looked to all of the ones watching from the branches, buzzing. Trees oranged on one side—algae, Mr Hardy told us, filaments of cells. A thing that tizzed got in my ear briefly then out. A glitter on things that God never believed in, it was hard to imagine it happening, any of this. The sleeping foxes, the hidden birds. Bristles, feathers, claws. Otters in the grass. Bats. Vs in the air. Tufts of fleece on twigs. The heart of a human being buried in the earth. Feeling the end of a pulse, the finish of it in the ends of our fingers. Last words. The hair still growing. That last day I thought I was being followed by the cats or others. I walked away, desperate but quite glad, looking forward to the train. I would put my head against the window and sleep and be bumped awake and fall asleep again. Deliciously inert. Then I'll always remember this. I looked down at my feet on the path and saw a wasp washing his body in the dust, right there ahead, before flying off, half-asleep. Wops. He bumped against me and then went away. I was amazed! But kept on walking.

I posted the letter, bought a loaf of bread for our lunch, then arrived at my mother's house, whereupon seeing her, I rushed into her arms and fell against her weeping and weeping. Arlright, me blebber, arlright.

Mrs Florence wrote to me when she got to London. Dear Nellie, I wish to offer you a position. It will just be the two of us since the place is a flat with a series of rooms and not a separate house. The views are splendid, looking over the Thames, the electric signs along the Embankment. Even the whisky advertisement of a Scots soldier in full uniform, she wrote, is charming. It was in the same building as Sir James. Indeed she was nursing him. She wrote of his bronchitis, his agonising chest, and that the doctor's prescription of heroin offered little relief. She was cooking Barrie his favourite meals: fish, cutlets, and apple tart and cream (made from Cook's old Dorset recipe). 'I think you'd all be proud of me,' she put.

I wrote back with the news that I was pregnant. I'd be unable to take up her kind offer. Then when I lost the baby, I wrote to her and asked if the position was still available. But it had been taken. She wished me luck and told me to call on her when I was next in London. Her book came out not too long after that. The biography that he'd dictated to her.

The baby wasn't Alex's.

I do think of that baby's life and possible futures we might have shared but then the thoughts dwindle quickly. I try not to let that slipping away happen but it does. Some subjects, it seems, can't be supported, even by acts of will.

I thought it was a girl.

Alice sent me a couple of letters. She was with a family in Cornwall who were mad and disorganised but she was sorting them out, she said. In the next letter she was engaged to a chap who worked in a garage ('boring') and who had a small boat he sailed ('romantic') and they were planning to escape to Canada or somewhere, though not on the small boat ('dangerous but you knew that'). I wrote back but never heard from her again. Her second letter hadn't replied to any of my news or my questions so perhaps she thought I'd never received her first one, and gave up. One thing she knew: a girl she worked with had some association with the place James Barrie lived and had told her that Florence Hardy had been humiliated by Barrie. 'No details,' Alice wrote, 'but we can imagine the hideous worst for that sad stunty pair!'

I heard from my mother that Florence Hardy had returned to Max Gate but was living in a very different way to how things had been with Thomas Hardy. Ma had spoken to someone—of course. The house was light now, with the trees cut back, and fitted with all the modern conveniences. Florence had also become a generous supporter of town renewal and was the driving force behind housing improvements in the slums of Mill Street in Dorchester. She was a rich woman who, by all accounts, wanted little for herself.

Bert Stephens slipped from view—Ma knew nothing of him. During the War, Ma read in the paper that Alex Peters had been killed. He was featured as an ex-journalist of the paper, with a photo from around the time I knew him. Ma sent me the clipping, which I no longer have. It failed to mention any connection with Thomas Hardy. It was so terribly sad. I regretted how we'd parted. How I'd walked away from the graveyard and never seen him again.

I remember now: a man from Dorchester came every Monday to wind the three clocks at Max Gate. No one else was allowed to touch them. This man was the person Ma knew and who gave her the information she always craved.

A few years later, when Florence was dying, she moved her bed downstairs to save everyone the nuisance of going up and down the stairs.

Of course she was assured of a spot at Stinsford when still his secretary. He'd taken her there when she was a young woman and pointed at the spot. When Alice heard that she said, These people are like ghosts.

But Florence was no ghost in those last years. At her Stinsford funeral, attended by many, certainly Hardy's presence was strong, as it had to be. Among the beautiful wreaths, a model of his birthplace, the cottage at Bockhampton, made of autumn leaves. But there was also a group of more recent friends and grateful beneficiaries, including the officials and tenants of the Mill Street Housing Society, which Florence had chaired and to which she'd made such an energetic contribution. Was this the most powerful tribute? I imagine it so. From the tenants of every house she'd helped build, a flower from the garden; and all these flowers forming the shape of a chair. Because of course she'd been the Chair. Yet this floral object, empty and carried into the church—it meant, I feel, something more than 'Sit down now. Here is your rest.' Did it not also say: 'This is the simple, unlikely place from which so much originated! Look: This is the driver's seat.'

Something else: F. put in a sundial, fixed to the house, designed by him of course. Making the house complete.

Developments I remember Ma remarking on and then I saw them myself: Bockhampton Heath planted in pines. The old network of sluice ditches running from the water meadows, empty and dry.

If you walk the narrow, chalky paths near the Rushy Pond, do you still see the flints? The ants' nests?

The crinkled waters of the Frome. The blue path across the meadows.

*

This: up on the roof with Alice. A glorious night, warm and vivid. We can see the reflections of lights from the town. I'm telling her a strange story I've thought about ever since. One evening, in my first year of employment, I was walking back to Max Gate having completed some errand. As we all did, I walked in the middle of the road. I came around a corner, still about half a mile from the house, and there were two men sitting on chairs on either side of the road. They were looking at each other. But what were they doing? Alice asked. Nothing, I told her. They were just sitting there, staring. And did you know them? No, I'd never seen them before. How old? Don't know, not young, I think. But it was too dark to tell. Sitting on chairs makes them sound old but I don't know. What did ye do? I ran. I ran between them—I mean I crossed the line that went from one side of the road to the other, from one man to the other. When I passed them, for a second, I thought they might have placed a rope or some thing to trip me and catch me—a net or something, which was invisible. My feet would trip or the thin twine would slice my neck. I shut my eyes at that moment. But, Alice said, but how horrible and terrifying! Yes, I said. It was the most terrifying thing I've ever come across. I ran all the way back here.

Alice disliked me telling the story as much as I hated thinking about it. Yet I'd told it. We tell stories to get rid of them. Does it work? She said: But who were they? What were they doing sitting on chairs? Don't know. Why would they have been there? What possible reason would there have been? I don't know—maybe they were just out to scare folk. By sitting all night by the side of the road? And why didn't they leap up when you passed, Nellie? Wouldn't it have been easier to jump out at ye from the bushes? Give ye a real scare like that? Maybe, but this—this was scarier still. This was scarier than saying boo. I know it's scarier, she said. Fuck me, I know it is and it makes me think ye couldn't have made it up, Nell. Because if you were making fac stuff up, you'd just have had them jump out at ye. I'm not making it up, I said. Thank ye very fucking much, she said. We didn't speak for several moments and then she said, You'll have to tell me something else now because I'm not going to bed with fac in my head.

I take a breath.

Dearest Robert lies where we left him. Funny that. It's not Robert really, more Robot. I don't mean the 'spirit has departed leaving the outer shell', though this is true too, but more that he's not much like himself—even the shell isn't quite right. The minute we brought him home and Jenny held my hand and gasped, I knew we'd done the wrong thing. His face is a waxy rectangle (wrong shape). The mouth is prim (wrong set). The hair flat—I was going to say lifeless. Benjamin said, He looks like he's thinking of something. And that is exactly it. He looks like he is thinking of something but lacks a brain and so the effort seems—I was going to say pointless. It's not the soul that leaves, it's the mind. Yet all through yesterday friends and relations came to the house and, having sat with me for a few minutes, told us that they were comforted by seeing him here, surrounded by familiar objects. A couple of the younger ones were distraught when they arrived but emerged calm from the room having been with the body. And I asked Benjamin what he thought Robert was thinking. 'He's probably thinking, I wonder if they've remembered to water my tomatoes.'

I hear noises outside. Really this storm is an utterly futile happening in my life as I'm living it, pretending to.

All night dreaming of Max Gate. All those hours with the wrong story, the wrong man, the wrong life. Wrong in so many details too, I realise now. The dog of course didn't wait for his master to go first. Wessex died two years before. I remember Hardy coming to us and saying, 'He sleeps outside the house tonight for the first time in thirteen years.' Why did I make the creature keep vigil outside the dying man's door? Why imagine him leaping to bite the pillows on Florence's bed? What else from this night was wrong? Yet yet—.

Hardy in company never let the conversation stop. Never disdained small talk and his quizzical eyes would grow bright with the conversation. His shrewd smile. Dressed in his rough grey jacket and striped tie. His nose with that joint in it and the end curved down. His round whitish face. His vigour, sitting on his three-cornered chair. His hunger for facts, incidents. Freedom, ease, vitality. He leans forward to speak to the visitor, a woman much younger than he is—I remember your father…

Never let the conversation stop.

Ugh, these tears! Thought I'd seen the last of them.

In the conservatory, resentfully, I pull the curtains and

look into the garden. There are my neighbours, clad in bright parkas and woolly hats—a young couple who left me a casserole on the back step two days ago—dragging the fallen branches into a neat pile near the back fence. How irritating. How wrong this pair is. If I tap on the glass, will they go away? Where are the foxes? But then I think: wonder how long my neighbours have been working? Miserable weather. The pile is massive. What kind kind people.

I can't bear to see what I've lost from the garden.

They see me and wave. What can I do, I wave back. I'm an old woman, grieving alone. I'm ancient, solo, sick of the universe, vaguely interested in a cup of tea. I'm the victim of a tempest. I'm a mother and a grandmother. Widow. Which is too close to window. What do we do? We wave. Stand at the window and wave to kind people. Come in, we say. Come in after you've finished. Then what? Maybe just to have something to do, I put one hand in my dressing-gown pocket. Which is when I remember. Last night, or in the early morning, unable to sleep, I found myself in the garage, looking through boxes. The storms must have passed. The tree surgery winds. The immense rushing of forces, the splintering of any obstacles in their path. I'd already gone through the storage cupboard in the spare room. I was on a hunt and almost ready to give up. Anyone coming across me might have thought I was sleepwalking. I was in the world and I was just above it. I was driven but also floating. I was thinking about Florence Hardy finding Tom's bed empty, his body gone and the great relief of having that sorted. Checking again before returning to her bed. Ah good. At certain points in my search I had no idea what I was after. Was it that book Florence gave me about the two children in the garden? I think I probably did nod off a couple of times while standing up. Then finally.

No memory of getting back to the bedroom. Lucky I didn't brain myself on the stairs.

But look here, I have it yet, forgive me, the thing I took when I was hardly more than a girl in the eye of an old man trying to remember something, either from his past or from a time he'd only imagined: Thomas Hardy's bicycle clip, still with spring in it, still, I have to say, squeezing it in my hand, alive. Put it on your leg and it's as though someone has reached down and gripped you in that tender place above the ankle. Ride, they tell you, yet they are holding you in place. Ride—and finally you do.

Author's Note

The idea for this novel came from reading Hardy's last novel *Jude the Obscure* and then from learning about his life. Alongside the various Hardy biographies (Michael Millgate, Ralph Pite, Claire Tomalin) and books about J. M. Barrie (Andrew Birkin, Lisa Chaney, Piers Dudgeon), I found information, inspiration and oddness in a variety of online sources, including The London Dog Forum Ltd, The British Newspaper Archive, Dorset Dialect, and Dorset Ancestors, where I came across the real Nellie Titterington. There are passages and phrases in the novel from *The Collected Letters of Thomas Hardy* (Oxford University Press) as well as from Florence Hardy's book about her husband, which he dictated to her. *The Second Mrs Hardy* by Robert Gittings and Jo Manton was also invaluable, as was *Some Recollections* by Emma Hardy. All the poems attributed to Hardy can be found in *Selected Poems* (Oxford Poetry Library, Robert Mezey, ed.). The speech Alex makes on page 170 is lifted from *Far From the Madding Crowd*, chapter 24. I took the word 'lammigers', which Alice uses on page 164, from chapter 39 of *The Mayor of Casterbridge*. According to the *OED*, except for being recorded in an 1847 *Dictionary of Archaic and Provincial Words*, its only appearance is in Hardy's novel. It means 'a lame person, a cripple' (*Oxford English Dictionary*).

This novel takes liberties with the historical record and comfort in the fact that T. H. was not above creating the deception that his wife was the author of the first posthumous book about his life.

D. W.

Reading group questions

To what extent is *Max Gate* a novel about Thomas Hardy? How does Hardy come across in the book?

Why do you think writers choose to fictionalise the lives of famous people, especially fellow authors?

Writer Michelle de Kretser described the novel as 'superbly attuned to that tremulous moment just before everything changes forever – the Hardy household, the known world of domestic servitude and dutiful women.' What does the book tell us about the wider society of the time, and women's role in it?

What do we learn about Hardy's relationship with his wives? Do you sympathise with Florence Hardy?

Why do you think Damien Wilkins chose to tell the story through the voice of a housemaid? Is Nellie a reliable narrator?

The novel has an unusual style, ranging from lyrical and abstract passages to coarse dialogue in local dialect. What effect does this varied approach have?

How important are nature and the animal kingdom in the book?

In an interview with the *New Zealand Herald*, Damien Wilkins said he was inspired by 'the scenario of who owns someone after they've gone'. How far is this a novel about ownership? And, in your opinion, was the right decision made regarding Hardy's final resting place?